JACK IN CLINK

A Jack of All Trades novel

DH Smith

Earlham Books

Published 2023 by Earlham Books
Book design & cover art by Lia at Free Your Words

ISBN: 978-1-909804-62-3

Chapter 1

It was dark on the Flats and Jack had set up his telescope. In a wheelbarrow, he'd pushed it from his van across the dark expanse. The area was never truly dark, with a fringe of cars and street lights a few hundred yards off in any direction, but it was the best he could do in his locality, short of driving fifteen miles to Epping Forest and completely dark skies.

The gloom and solitude suited his mood. Nova had kept him waiting fifteen minutes outside Stratford Picture House earlier that evening before texting to say she couldn't get away. He'd gone in alone to watch the film, but couldn't concentrate, arguing with Nova in his head. A relentless commentary where he always had the last word, but the words bounced back on himself.

He'd left the cinema after twenty minutes, the events in his head too powerful for those on the screen. So he phoned, catching her in pressured busyness. They'd had a row. Short but hard hitting. One of those shouty affairs, with passers-by looking at him strangely.

'I'm a detective,' she'd declared, 'I don't keep regular hours.'

'And I don't expect to be stood up,' he'd countered.

'I don't have the time for this, Jack.'

'Make time.' The decibels rising.

It ended when she suggested a month's cooling off. And he'd ended the call. A month could mean a month, or could mean forever.

Stood up and ditched, three hours ago.

A shooting star, a dart out of the black-blue. One of the Lyrids. Half a second of light, a streaking meteor, the size of

1

a sand grain, burning up in the atmosphere. And now another. The debris of a comet, every April, crossing the earth's orbit, appearing to come from the star Vega in the constellation Lyra.

Such knowledge calmed him. Space was reliable, if his personal life wasn't.

He gazed into the blueness, his eyes dark-adjusted. Sometimes you look and never see any shooting stars. And other times, they come continuously. Tonight, a welcome surprise. And there, Leo, just to the south west. Like old friends, come to offer sympathy.

His telescope was focussed on the moon. A half moon, quite high in the southern sky, centred on the crater, Ptolemaeus, with the shadow of the terminator emphasising the rim...

Jack stepped back from his scope. Did she mean it? She could be savage. A cop has got to be tough, has to be able to wade into the melee. He knew he had a temper too. Why couldn't he have found someone with a nine to five job?

Was it love, or need? Was there a difference?

Another shooting star. A bright spark, out in an instant. Like ourselves, full of self importance and gone in a flash. Philosophical under the stars.

Behind him was a copse of trees in new leaf, a dark outline occluding that area of night sky. But he was looking south, across the plane, up at the moon which was above the line of trees on the edge of the Flats.

The veils of passion stripped away, as he looked up into the universe, where no one cared, loved or hated, beautiful indifference to a lone builder on Wanstead Flats. He must eat. The stars would still be there after a mouthful. His anger and unhappiness had pushed away thoughts of food, but with his diabetes he couldn't afford to forget. His body wouldn't.

Jack went to get his backpack, stashed in the wheelbarrow...

A distant cry of help. Instantly, flushed in adrenaline, he searched out the direction of the appeal. Where was it? He could make out nothing. It came again.

'Help me! Help me!'

A male voice, from a sort of southerly direction.

Jack ran towards the cries. They ceased. He slowed, realising he didn't know what he might be running into. A gun, a knife, a gang? He walked swiftly, eyes peering into the darkness.

There was someone running, a hundred metres away, a negative of a shooting star, black on purple, and gone as quickly.

Jack almost tripped over the lump of a person, laid out on the short grass, unmoving like a long sack. He dropped to his knees and shone his phone. A man, balding, in a white shirt stained with blood, jeans, portly, mouth agape.

Alive or dead? Near dead at least, with all that blood, a shapeless island, covering much of the shirt. He shone the phone into the man's face, and rocked back with shock. It couldn't be. Not possible.

A car was driving away, he could hear but not see. The killer? Or lovers needing to get home.

He turned back to the body. Tom Litt. His client, believe that, of all people, his client, here in the solitude of the Flats. What was the odds?

Jack phoned 999.

'What service do you require?'

'Police,' then a thought, 'and ambulance. There's a man on Wanstead Flats, dead I think, but I'm not sure.'

Jack was put through to the police. He told them where he was as clearly as possible. He was told to stay there until they arrived, then put through to the ambulance service.

'Is the patient breathing?'

Jack put his hand over the open mouth. The police had asked the same question.

'I can't feel any air going in or out. He's covered in blood.'

'Have you tried mouth to mouth?'

'The police told me not to touch him.'

'Feel his forehead. Is he cold?'

Jack put his hand on the clammy forehead. Like a piece of meat.

'It's cold.'

'Put your hand under his shirt. Is there any warmth?'

Jack undid a couple of buttons in the bloody island of shirt. His fingers becoming sticky, he opened the shirt and pressed a palm against the man's chest.

'Not much.' Was there any? He was too agitated to be sure.

'Thank you. We're on our way.'

Left to silence and darkness, having done his duty with cops and medicos, Jack was shivering through his padded jacket, scarf and woolly hat.

Calm down. He began breathing steadily, counting each breath. He must eat.

His telescope!

His most valued possession, he couldn't just leave it out there. He strode off, knowing more or less where it was, thinking as he ran, his client dead, is that the end of the job? He'd had part payment but was owed £800 odd.

Tom Litt of all people.

Jack didn't like him much. Fussy and picky, standing over and watching as he laid bricks, not Jack's strongest area anyway. His wife was OK, made him tea, chatted a bit but just about the work. It was obvious Tom didn't like her talking to him. Tom was the boss, a jealous one.

Would she take over and pay him what he was owed? Would the work go on?

Hardly the right thoughts for a grieving widow. His needs were not hers.

He loaded the telescope on its mount into the wheelbarrow. He'd disassemble it when he was back at the body. No-one would know he'd left the corpse for a few minutes. He took up the handles and headed back, bumping along the grass, breathing heavily.

He was hot, shivering. Like a fever.

There was a siren, coming closer. He had to be back before the cops arrived or he'd have awkward questions to answer, but no way could he leave 600 quid's worth of telescope by itself.

He increased speed as the siren drew closer. He stopped, looked about. Where was the body?

Jack scoured the area. Got out his phone. There, maybe 50 yards away.

He covered them rapidly, and let go of the wheelbarrow. His hands went to his hips, bending forward, gasping. He hadn't eaten, but with a corpse, could his stomach hold anything?

Must try.

His mouth was full of banana when the police arrived.

A middle-aged woman in a dark dress suit holding a torch was approaching with two uniformed cops. Jack gulped the banana, the skin in his hand he thrust in his pocket. He was eager to get away, to eat and be out of sight of the corpse of his client.

The woman stopped at the scene, clearly in charge, the two uniforms behind her awaiting instructions. She was almost Jack's height, her hair a cloche cut. She shone her torch on the body and then at Jack, dazzling him.

'And you are?' she said.

'Jack Bell. I found him.'

'Detective Inspector Kate Hawley,' she said by way of introduction. 'And what, may I ask, Mr Bell, were you doing on the Flats this time of night?'

He bridled, somewhat knocked back by her approach. Having to defend himself for being the good citizen. She was glaring at him, sizing him up, like a head teacher at a miscreant.

'I was out with my telescope,' he said, indicating the wheelbarrow. 'It's a good night for stargazing.'

Another siren was homing in. More cops or paramedics?

'So you came across the body... How, may I ask? The Flats are extensive.' She had hands on hips, a woman who took no prisoners.

'I heard a cry for help. So I came over...'

'But your telescope is here, Mr Bell. Not out there.' She waved an arm, indicating the far Flats.

'While I was waiting for you,' he said, 'I went off to get it. Not wanting to leave it out there unattended.'

She sighed heavily. 'Contaminating the crime scene with your coming and going. Great start. What else? Have you touched the body?'

'The ambulance service told me to feel his forehead and chest to find out if he was still warm.'

She held up a warning hand. 'Enough, sir. You will have to be fingerprinted and your DNA taken.'

'He might have been alive, Inspector.'

'Detective Inspector.' She corrected him and shrugged. 'Can't be helped. You weren't to know, I suppose.'

Know what? he thought. That the man was alive or dead? And touching him was contamination. She was determined to put him in the wrong, as if only the police should find bodies and touch them in search for life. He was off the cops big time. Irrational maybe, but he was hungry and belittled. First Nova and her cooling off, now this officious woman. They make it their business to blame you for something. Anything, just to be superior.

She was talking to her colleagues. He caught the words 'crime scene' and 'pathologist'. One of the uniforms went off, speaking on the phone as he strode away.

Two paramedics in overalls were walking quickly towards them, a man holding a bright torch and woman hefting a large bag.

'Is he alive?' said the woman as she got to them.

'Dead,' said DI Hawley.

'I'll check.'

She knelt down.

'Can you check without touching him?'

'No.'

Jack felt vindicated, as the paramedic felt his forehead, checked his chest, his mouth. She stood up.

'He's been dead a while,' she said.

'How long?' said DI Hawley.

The paramedic shrugged. 'Don't know. That's your job, and I reckon that's a bullet wound. I've seen too many of those.' She turned to her colleague. 'There's nothing we can do here. Let's go.' And then to DI Hawley. 'All yours, ma'am.'

She nodded to her fellow paramedic, who nodded back. They left the scene.

The detective inspector watched them on their way, as if annoyed at them for some reason. Or was she always this way? The uniform who'd been on the phone came over.

'Crime Scene is on the way, and the pathologist.'

'Let's all back off,' she said. 'And not contaminate the scene any more than we already have.'

She directed them back several metres. Jack was feeling a little useless. He wanted to go home. He'd done his duty. Only one thing left to do, then he could be away from this officious cop.

'His name is Tom Litt,' he said.

'What!' she turned on him, affronted. 'You know him? And you didn't say!'

He didn't want to say, I'm hungry, I'm tired, I'm not used to finding bodies. And I don't like you.

'He's my client,' he said, keeping back his irritation. 'I'm a builder, working on a job at his house.'

She peered at him, eyes half closed. 'And you just happened to find him dead on the Flats?'

'Yes.' It was sounding suspicious even to him.

'That's somewhat of a coincidence,' she said.

'Yes.' What else could he say? It was.

'And you heard cries for help? From a dead man?'

'I heard cries for help,' he said.

She lifted her phone and snapped a photo of him.

'I'd like to see some ID.'

Jack sighed heavily and searched his pockets. He brought out an envelope. It had his name and address on. He handed it over.

'Inside is an invoice for building materials.'

She looked at the envelope and took the invoice out, perusing it. Then looked him up and down, obviously contemplating her next step.

'Give me your phone, Mr Bell.'

'Why?'

'Your story is fishy. Give me your phone or I will arrest you.'

He was astounded, seeing the way this was heading.

'I found him,' he declared, 'and like a good citizen called the police.'

'Phone, please.' She held out her hand as if he hadn't spoken. Jack reluctantly handed it over. 'Have you a vehicle?'

'A van, Jack of All Trades, on the road back there.' He pointed.

'Give me the keys.'

'You're joking.'

'Give me the keys.'

Jack hesitated.

'This is my last warning, Mr Bell. Give me the keys, or I will arrest you. And for that matter, I will be keeping your wheelbarrow and telescope for the time being, as part of the crime scene.'

Chapter 2

Jack walked through Forest Gate, back into the land of traffic and street lights, in disbelief at what had happened back on the Flats. He wasn't expecting a medal, but she hadn't even allowed him his backpack. 'Crime scene,' she'd snapped, and ordered him to come into the station in the morning to give a statement.

He was shaky, hollow-legged, due to lack of food, finding a body and the heavy hand of the law. If he'd left the body and phoned anonymously from a call box... But no, he'd been a good guy, and waited for the law to arrive. Well, almost waited, going to get his telescope, taking just a few minutes. What did she expect of him? To leave a six hundred pounds instrument for any taker?

Obviously.

Jack was aware he hadn't thought of Nova for half an hour. A worse cop than her had taken centre stage. He crossed at the lights to Forest Gate station, the Co-op next door was shuttered. Would be. He glanced at his watch, at least she hadn't taken that. Ten minutes to midnight. He'd like some chips, but it was quicker to get home then wait to be served. Besides which, he wasn't sure how much he had on his credit card, and didn't want that hassle at the counter. There was enough in his kitchen cupboard for once.

It hit him as he turned into Earlham Grove, like a punch in the guts. He was tottering like a drunk. On one foot, and hardly making next step, like a top heavy infant. Jack rested against the railings of the community garden. Breathe, in and out, steadily. Count. Grip fists. He knew what was likely coming. He'd faint. A diabetic collapse. Eat regularly, he'd been told often enough. And he'd had food with him. Back in the wheelbarrow, now with Madam Dracula.

Jack walked on, resting against walls as he proceeded. Only a hundred yards to home and food. A man approached, watching him, and giving a wide berth as if Jack was sloshed.

He staggered on and stopped at a tree. The world was twisting in giddiness. He wasn't going to make it. Fifty yards, but it seemed miles. Stupid. He'd prepared for this, but not for a body. His brain was seeking sugar urgently, his bloodstream clear of it. Goodbye and goodnight.

'Dad!'

He turned groggily, only half making out Mia. She was in her school uniform, with her backpack on her shoulders. Was she real?

Was this a coma dream?

'What you doing here?' he managed to say, leaning on the tree, treating the apparition as real.

'Had a row with Mum. I'll tell you later.' She was peering at him in concern.

She was real. Really real.

'What's happened to you?' she said.

'Tell you later.' He held out a shaky hand in appeal. 'Got any food?'

Mia took off her backpack, searched inside and handed him half a bottle of 7-UP. Jack glugged it down like an eager baby, feeling energy swelling through his body. Junk drink, full of all the wrong stuff, just what he needed right now.

She handed him two thirds of a bar of chocolate.

'I'll remember you in my will,' he said as he broke off the cubes and munched away.

'A second-hand van and a load of tools,' she said with a half laugh. 'Thank you very much.'

She was almost as tall as he was, lots of dark brown curly hair. He didn't like her being out so late, in spite of his gratitude.

He put a hand in his pocket. There was a soggy banana skin but not what he was looking for. He tried the other pocket.

'I haven't got my door keys,' he said.

'How come?'

'They're with my car keys. Had to give them to a cop. Didn't think, I was so mad at her for taking my phone and telescope.'

Mia shook her head in concern. 'If I hadn't come, you might have been found dead on the doorstep.' She looked him up and down. 'You OK to walk?'

Jack left the support of the tree. The world was stable again. He was weak but the giddiness had gone.

'You've got to take care,' she said.

She took his arm, and they walked home.

Chapter 3

Mia sat her father at the kitchen table while she made him tea and scrambled eggs on toast. She had toast and black tea, skipping the egg as she was 'half vegan'. He enquired no more on this as he'd had enough lectures from her on his own diet and on the needless slaughter of animals.

He concentrated on eating.

'You found a body,' she said. 'Why doesn't that surprise me?'

'You sound like your mother.' He stopped shovelling in food, and took a swig of tea. 'And I nearly got arrested for it.'

'That's standard with cops. Did they have any grounds? Not that they ever need any.'

He was familiar with her attitude to the police since she'd become an eco-warrior. Or eco-worrier as her mother phrased it.

'The body was the guy I'm working for.'

Mia widened her eyes. 'Some coincidence.'

'That's what the detective said. See, you and the cops are not always in disagreement.'

She blew a raspberry at him. He forked up some eggy toast, feeling almost human. All grogginess had gone, the world sort of made sense, or as much as it ever did.

'Me and the detective lady just didn't hit it off,' he said, and it struck him as he was saying this, how it might affect an arrest, whether you and the cop got on. Prejudice. He wasn't black but then again he was out doing weird things on the Flats late at night.

'She took my van keys, my phone, my wheelbarrow with my telescope and backpack.'

'She could have killed you,' Mia protested. 'Taking your grub. Just think if I hadn't come along, if me and Mum hadn't had a row.'

'Detective Inspector Kate Hawley,' he said with some vehemence. 'She was ticking the boxes with me as the killer. Cops! I get you sometimes. Can you trust 'em when it comes to the crunch?'

'You're going out with one. Remember?'

'Was. Nova stood me up at the Picture House. I phoned, we had a row. And now we are cooling off for a month.'

Mia sniggered as she munched her toast.

'Never really liked her,' she said. 'I tried for your sake, but I was always careful about what I said to her. Take that as a lesson. You can't trust 'em, as you found out tonight. Twice.'

'I can't blame Nova for detective Dracula. Much as I'd like to.'

'They're all the same type,' she said. 'Instruments of the state. We see it on our demos. They stop you randomly, kettle you, accuse you of whatever, beat you up and lie about everything.'

Jack had heard this line before. Her anti-cop tirade. Pointless arguing, as he wasn't feeling at one with the city's law enforcers. But Nova was a woman as well as a cop, and that was the trouble. If she'd only met him at the Picture House, he wouldn't be thinking this way. Or have met detective Dracula for that matter. Or have phoned in the corpse.

Or collapsed on the street.

All Nova's fault. Everything. Original sin, evil in the world, it all emanated from her.

And he wished she were here.

But they were cooling off. Accept it, live with it. Eat and be merry. Focus on something else.

'So why are you here anyway?' he said to Mia.

'Me and Mum had a row, like I said. Not unusual. There's a big demo tomorrow, we're picketing Parliament, and she said I couldn't go because of school, blah, blah. So I walked out and came round here. Lucky I did.'

What was he to say? She was 17, she was taking a day off school. He couldn't imprison her.

'Climate change is a human induced catastrophe,' she went on. 'And Mum wants me in school like nothing's happening. We could be wiped out. The human race done with. Our government is doing nothing. Got all the words but no action. They all have shares in oil companies.'

'You don't know that.'

'I do, I tell you.' She was getting fierce, wearing her eco-warrior's hairshirt. 'You see how many MPs and cabinet ministers are lobbyists for Big Oil, for Saudi Arabia and the Gulf...'

'Some is not all.'

'You can talk, with your shaky old van belching out more CO2 than a coal power station.'

She tended to exaggerate, but he couldn't say she was wrong, not the way the world was going. Just a little over the top.

'Don't get arrested,' he said.

'Can't exactly stop them if they want to do it. They put on the uniform and switch off their brains. Your Nova too, as if she won't be a victim of climate change. They'll toss you into the paddy wagon, no excuses needed.'

He held up his palms.

'Enough. I've had more than my fill tonight. Don't add to it.'

'Sorry.'

They were silent a while. He felt stronger, but it had been a close call. Too close. He looked at his daughter, putting marmalade on her toast. Her head abuzz with saving the planet, annoying her head teacher of a mother. Mia was becoming her own woman. How could it be otherwise?

'What are you doing tomorrow?' she said.

He sighed at the thought of tomorrow's timetable. 'I have to go to the cop shop and make a statement. I hope DI Dracula isn't there.'

'You might see Nova there.'

Or his mate Fayyad, he thought. A cop he did like.

'Then I'll be going to my client's house,' he continued. 'Former client's house. I'm dreading that. I'll tell his wife how sorry I am about the death of her husband. I don't know how she'll react. They must have told her by now. I'll ask her if she still wants me working on the job, and, more importantly, if she is going to pay me.'

'That sounds worrying.'

'Tom Litt owed me £800. I won't get paid tomorrow, I'm sure of that, but I've got to put the invoice in. OK, I'll delay it a few days, but I can't afford to hold it longer.' He stopped. 'You got enough for lunch tomorrow?'

'Still got most of my birthday money.'

'That's OK then.'

He rose.

'I've had more than enough for one day, and it's heading for one o'clock. Let's get some shut eye.'

Chapter 4

Jack didn't sleep well. Mia had the bedroom, he had the couch. That was the routine when she came over. The couch wasn't the problem, he was accustomed to that. It was finding the body, the hostile detective, mingled with thoughts of Nova. He didn't want to 'cool off'. He sort of loved her, some of the time, though not when she stood him up. Did it mean they could never arrange a date?

Did it mean the end? Relationship after relationship. They all hit the buffers sooner or later.

Nothing could be sorted out at two in the morning, it was senseless going over and over the row on the phone, the temporary loss of the van and his telescope. That hurt, the loss of the telescope. It was like a teddy bear, Alison, his ex, said. She'd called it 'a boy's toy'. So what? Now he was having a row with her in the early hours, shape shifting from Alison to detective Dracula and her avatar Nova...

How not to get to sleep.

Somehow, in the witching hour between three and four, his arguing head surrendered and he dropped off. Into quiet and silence. Into oblivion.

He was rudely awakened by someone shaking him. For a few seconds he pushed the brusque hands away. His name was being called. No dream. What on earth...

'Wake up, Mr Bell.'

Standing over him was detective Dracula and two uniformed police officers.

He sat up, wiping his eyes.

'What are you doing here? How did you get in?'

DI Hawley held up his front door keys.

She said, 'Jack Bell, I am arresting you for the murder of Tom Litt. You do not have to say anything, but it may harm your defence if you do not mention when questioned something which you later rely on in court. Anything you do say may be given in evidence.' Mia came out of the bedroom, barefoot in her dressing gown, her hair tousled.

'What's going on?'

Jack was fully awake, the adrenalin rush a bucket of cold water.

'I'm being arrested for murder,' he said to his daughter. 'A massive mistake. You are wasting your time with me, Inspector.'

'Please get dressed,' said DI Hawley. 'We are taking you to the station. Put on the clothes you were wearing yesterday. These, I assume?'

She pointed to the untidy pile on a chair. Jack nodded. He rose, in his underwear, and began dressing in yesterday's gear.

'He didn't do it!' yelled Mia.

'Please be quiet, young lady. We have sufficient evidence to warrant his arrest. If he is innocent, he can make his case. But be assured, I wouldn't be charging him if the evidence against him wasn't strong.'

'He's being set up!' yelled Mia. 'My father is not a killer.'

Jack put on his socks and shoes. DI Hawley was gazing at the picture on her phone of Jack on the Flats. She looked him up and down, referring back to the photo.

'And the jacket and scarf you were wearing last night.'

Jack took them off the hook on the door and put them on.

'It's a load of cobblers, all this,' he mumbled. 'You are so wrong. I don't know who has been telling you what, but it's rubbish.' He turned to Mia. 'Phone your mother. Phone Nova. Tell them I have been arrested.' He turned back to DI Hawley. 'Where are you taking me?'

'Forest Gate police station.'

She snapped handcuffs onto his wrists.

Chapter 5

It was a few minutes drive to the police station, four in the same car, Jack and three police officers. He was in the back, handcuffed, with a policeman at his side. It was light, the rush hour just beginning.

This was a nightmare. He'd wake up soon. They'd realise their mistake.

Jack watched the people at a bus stop, free to come and go, free as work allows. At a set of traffic lights, he was stared at by a young woman driver. Not that his handcuffs would be visible, but he was in the back seat with a uniformed officer. What would she say when she got to work?

'I saw this man in a cop's car, under arrest. He had a really evil face.'

Jack didn't speak on the short ride, as he knew the answers he'd get. Made concrete by the handcuffs and the caution he'd been given. All a mistake, laughable, it would all be sorted out in an hour or two. Above all, don't kick out or swear at the cops. Don't try a runner.

Take it step by step. Don't antagonise them. It will be sorted out, he told himself.

They drove into the station yard. Jack was led into the building through the back door, along a corridor and into a large room with an officer behind a counter. He was introduced as the custody sergeant.

Jack was taken to the back of the room while DI Hawley spoke to the custody sergeant in a low voice. He couldn't hear but could see the sergeant nodding. He guessed she was saying why he had been arrested, and the duty officer was assenting to the points she was making.

Jack was brought forward.

He was ordered to empty his pockets. Not that there was much in them. A few coins, a credit card, a couple of scrunched up tissues, two screws and an allen key for his telescope. It was bagged up, and he signed for it as if it were precious.

Jack's personal details were taken: full name, address, date of birth, next of kin. He didn't want his mother brought into this, feeling some shame in spite of his innocence, as he knew for many people being arrested meant guilty.

They asked if he had any health issues.

'I have type 2 diabetes,' he said. 'I have to eat regularly.'

He was told he'd be given breakfast once this procedure was over. A couple of times, Jack protested his innocence. This was handled routinely and politely, as if everyone gave the same spiel on arrest. There were five in the room other than himself, and he could see the uselessness of protesting or attempting to escape. He didn't know where he was in the police station, and numbers were against him.

'Do you want to see the duty solicitor?' asked the custody sergeant.

Half of him thought, what's the point? I'm innocent, they'll see that soon enough. The other half thought, maybe they won't. And he assented. At least the solicitor wasn't a cop, and might believe him.

The handcuffs were taken off and Jack was taken into a side room. There he was photographed, his fingerprints taken on a machine and a swab taken from his inside cheek for DNA purposes. Both hands were swabbed, backs and fronts, the inside of his fingers and fingernails.

'What's this for?' he asked.

'Routine,' said the officer.

Jack thought, I don't believe it. But there was a lot he didn't believe this morning, beginning with his wake up call and caution. Mia would have phoned her mother, Alison, and Nova, so at least he wasn't disappearing from outside help.

A sample of blood was taken. 'Routine' was the reply when he asked why. He was beginning to think if he was kicked and accidentally pushed down the stairs, 'routine' would be the pronouncement. It was their bat, their ball, their pitch. They were the umpire with the whistle and the flag.

Jack was taken into a locker room by two male officers. There, he was ordered to strip. He protested at the needlessness, and was told he could either do so willingly or by force.

Jack undressed to his underwear. Every item, he was told. He took off his vest and pants. All his clothing, including shoes, were put into a large plastic bag which was carefully labelled, while he stood naked. He knew taking clothes away was routine in authoritarian regimes to reinforce the feeling of helplessness.

All a game, he told himself. They will see it's a massive mistake. Mistaken identity. Keep your cool, stark naked or otherwise. They'll get there eventually. Like an ocean liner that takes miles to stop.

Enjoy the ride. And other inanities. He had no reason whatsoever to kill Tom Litt.

So why did they think he did?

An officer entered with a plastic box full of clothing. Jack was told to dress. The items looked more or less clean, though he wondered how many others had worn them. Murderers, rapists, child molesters, wife beaters. The guilty and the innocent before him, standing here in their birthday suits, the fat and thin, black, white and brown, trying to work out what the cops knew and what they didn't.

He put on boxer shorts and a vest, and felt he'd joined at least a subspecies of the human race. No one had treated him badly in the police station, but he felt demeaned and weak. All in less than an hour from when he had been rudely awoken.

It took little time for Jack to dress. Over the underwear, he put on loose, grey tracksuit bottoms and a more or less matching top with the sleeves too long. On his feet, he put on flip flops, no socks.

Jack was taken to a cell and locked in.

Chapter 6

The cell was basic. A platform against the wall, which functioned as a seat and a bed, though there was no blanket or pillow. Presumably those would be supplied if he was staying the night. Which he certainly wouldn't be. This all had to be an off-beam scenario in the mind of a cranky cop who would soon be shown how off-beam she was. There was a single chair, and a toilet at one end with a tiny sink. The walls were a pale green, with a fluorescent striplight in the ceiling. No window. A box in essence for human rats. All it needed was an exercise wheel.

They must be able to see him. Yes, there was a camera, like one of those reality TV shows. This one designed for boredom, as there was little he could do to entertain any watcher.

Jack sat on the bench. He had nothing to read, watch or listen to, but the stream of his thoughts which flitted here and there like excited mayflies. He put his ear to the wall. No sound, though he had noted, just before he was shut in, there were four other cells. Were they occupied? Awaiting the jailer's timetable, heads buzzing like his own.

He went over what he knew, for the umpteenth time. Someone had cried for help while he was at his telescope, about to explore the crater Ptolemaeus. Jack had run, walked, in the direction of the distress call, and had found a body on the Flats. His employer Tom Litt. That was a weird coincidence, if it was one. Just before finding the corpse, he had glimpsed someone running off. Not a lot he could add to that. A human shape, black against the blue-black of the night. The body was cold, so the cry for help could only have been to draw him to the body. And, like a law abiding citizen, he had phoned the police.

Someone was setting him up. What else had they done? DI Hawley said the police had a strong case. So they must have more than this. What?

He had no inkling. He would find out soon enough, and hoped he could disprove it. Once he knew what they had on him. There was the frustration on a plate. His ignorance of what they knew, or thought they knew. Why on earth would he want to kill his client?

He laughed, he'd lose money on it. Then again, the cops must think he had a motive. Money, sex, madness – why else do people kill? He wasn't mad, there was no sex or money on offer, so far as he knew.

Too many missing pieces in this jigsaw.

Jack had been in the cell about an hour when a tray of breakfast was brought to him. It consisted of a small carton for one of Rice Crispies, a plastic bowl, a small plastic jug of milk, a plastic spoon, two slices of toast on a paper plate, margarine and marmalade for one, tea, and three sachets of sugar.

Not bad, he thought. If only he were hungry. Being charged with murder quite dulls the appetite. But he needed to eat and stay sharp, to hear what they had on him, and work out the holes in their evidence.

There was no knife, plastic or otherwise. Just in case, he might want to cut his throat or fight his way out of the police station like Errol Flynn on the battlements.

It must be about 8 am, he guessed, with no watch or outside light to guide him. Not that time mattered. They were the Time Lords, deciding what happens next and when. His only obligation was to wait to be called.

Was Mia going on her picket today? Her Dad was up for murder, did that supplant climate change? Though, what could she do for him anyway? He wished he had a phone. Quite what he could say beyond, 'Help! It wasn't me!'

But if they held him for any length of time then he would need outside help for sure.

Jack opened the Rice Crispies and poured on the milk. Snap, crackle, pop in the milk, which was slightly sour. He sugared the cereal and ate. A mechanical spooning, no enjoyment. It was fear; Jack was shivery with anticipation. He had no power whatsoever. Shut in a box, with no contact to the world outside.

DI Hawley said he was a murderer. She was sure of it. How could she be?

There were many cases, he knew, of innocent people being found guilty. A substandard investigation, poor defence lawyer versus a hungry young prosecutor, lying cops, supportive evidence suppressed. He'd seen them on the news, found innocent after fifteen years imprisonment, protesting on the court steps how their life had been taken away.

He oscillated as he ate, from despair to the feeling that it would be seen to be a slip-up, mistaken identity, or not believing in the coincidence of his client being the victim, and then, finally, accepting some coincidences are just that.

The tea was tepid, the toast hard, hardly softened by margarine and marmalade. He ate some, stopped, went back to it and chewed some more. It was like eating cardboard, his stomach nauseated by his dilemma.

He knew so little, while they were beavering away building an ironclad case against him. A vast industry of police officers and forensic experts, a beehive of one mind, out to get him while he ate toast in a cell. Without a phone, without even paper and pen,

How could you make this space more hospitable? A TV, except he knew he couldn't watch people playing games, or cop shows and sitcoms. All pointless. Music, perhaps, but his mind was everywhere, he was impatient, scared, bored, lonely.

Too bad, too bad. They would come for him in their time. 'Let him stew' - wasn't that what the cops said in TV shows? Though maybe they were just getting up, showering, having breakfast with their families, not sticking pins in him. He wasn't that important.

He thought of Nova. Mia must have phoned her by now. Would she just leave him to stew too? Feeling, she couldn't interfere with those above her in the ranks. Leave Jack to cool off in a cell.

What would he do, if their roles were reversed? All he could. He'd visit, listen to her. Do whatever she asked.

'So, Nova, what are you up to?' he said, looking to the tiny camera in the ceiling. Likely they didn't have sound, and likely wouldn't have heard anyway. They could bring in a lip reader.

And so what?

Some time later, a police officer opened the door.

'The duty solicitor is here for you.'

Jack was led along the corridor to a large room. It had a frosted window, though there were no shapes moving outside. There were pleasant, orange curtains, a sofa and an armchair. Some attempt had been made to keep it homely. He was, as they say, innocent until proven guilty. At one end of the sofa sat the duty solicitor with a large pad in front of him. He was a small middle-aged man in a navy suit, the trousers a little too long. He was balding, his face florid.

Jack recognised a drinker.

The solicitor introduced himself as Peter Stone and invited Jack to sit on the sofa.

Jack sat down.

'I'm innocent,' he said.

'That you may well be,' said Peter with a wry smile, waving his hands as if to ward off evil spirits. 'I'm not here to judge you, just to make sure you are treated fairly. That is my limit. You may be as guilty as sin, you may be absolutely innocent. I have no way of knowing.'

'You don't do any investigation?'

'None at all.' He opened his hands to show they were empty. No tricks, nothing up his sleeve.

'Could you contact Inspector Fayyad Kamani for me? Ask him to visit.'

'He's at this station?'

Jack nodded.

'I will.' Stone made a rapid note. 'You are about to be interviewed. If there's a question you'd rather not answer, you may say – no comment.'

'There's nothing I don't want to answer,' said Jack.

'You may find there is, Mr Bell.' He rapped the point home with his pen.

Peter Stone used his hands a lot, waving them, pointing, as if they were activated by his tongue.

'My advice, in a nutshell, is be polite. There is nothing to be gained by antagonising your questioners.'

'I shouldn't be here,' said Jack.

Peter Stone threw up his hands.

'I can't help you there. I have no magic wand. All I can do is make sure they don't bully you and they act correctly. If I put a hand on your knee during the interview, don't misjudge it,' he said with a slight smirk. 'I am asking you to consider for a few seconds, maybe say no comment.' Stone rose. 'I think that's about it, Jack. I am simply a temporary solicitor for you. You will need to get your own, but I'll be at your first interview.' He paused, and looked down at Jack who was still sitting. 'Is there anything you want to ask me?'

'What's going to happen to me?'

'You will be questioned at this police station, Mr Bell. Then, some time today, you will be taken to a prison. I don't know which one. There, with your solicitor, you can prepare your defence.'

'I don't know what they have against me.'

'Neither do I, Mr Bell. But if you are ready for the interview, we'll find out.'

Chapter 7

Jack was led into the interview room with the duty solicitor. It was a medium-sized room with no décor other than a table with a tape recorder at the wall side, and four chairs. There was a video camera attached to the ceiling, angled at the table where two police officers were seated. One he knew as his arresting officer, the other he didn't know. A uniformed police officer had come in with Jack and the solicitor, and now stood against the wall. Security presumably. But any altercation, and numbers would be in here in a flash, caught on camera and through the blackened glass in one wall, which he assumed was an observing room.

Jack and Stone were invited to sit down. They did so. His knee was trembling as if about to address a throng. He pressed his foot to the floor, his hand on the rebelling knee.

Stay cool. He breathed in and out, clenched and unclenched his fists. Not that he was aching for a fight. Not a fist one at least. The seat was hard, fixed to the floor for obvious reasons.

Do your worst, copper.

Detective Inspector Hawley turned on the tape recorder, gave the time and date and introduced herself and her fellow officer, Detective Constable Ben Alagia, a black man in a grey suit. Heavy set. Jack reckoned he could outrun him but not outfight him.

Peter Stone introduced himself as the duty solicitor, and Jack was asked his full name and address for the recording. He gave them both. So far, so good, he told himself, as the man without a parachute said at 5,000 feet.

He looked at DI Hawley, his nemesis, and held her gaze. She was wearing a white blouse, her grey jacket behind her on the chair. Her face was just-washed pinkish, her cloche haircut a little wet. Jack wondered if she had slept. Maybe she was used to all-nighters.

'Can you tell us why you were on Wanstead Flats last night, Mr Bell?'

She knew already, but this was the way it was done, a few easy questions and then the googly to mid wicket.

'I regularly come out with my telescope,' he said. 'It's the one place nearby that has a semblance of dark skies. Not that good, but better than driving 15 miles for a site.'

'How often do you go viewing?' She was glancing down at her notebook.

'Depends. If it's cloudy, not at all. Sometimes two or three times a week. Last night, the sky was about half clear, with good views of some stars and the moon.'

'Tell us what happened. In your own time.'

'I was set up for viewing the moon, when I heard a cry for help. Several times, a man I think, but I can't be sure. It sounded very distressed, so I headed to where it came from. I glimpsed someone running off.'

'A man or woman?'

'I don't know. Just a shadowy form in the dark. And I stumbled across the body. Almost tripped over it. He was splayed out, face up, blood on the chest. I shone my phone on him. It was my client, Tom Litt. Which utterly amazed me.'

'Quite a coincidence, Mr Bell.'

'Yes,' he said. 'But sometimes a coincidence is just a coincidence.'

'And more often, it is not,' she added with a slight smirk. 'Continue please.'

'You know all this,' he said with a sigh.

'For the record, Mr Bell.'

He nodded, nothing incriminating so far, except a coincidence.

'I phoned the ambulance and the police. The ambulance told me to check whether he was alive. He didn't seem to be breathing. I was told to feel his forehead, which was cold, and then his chest. I undid his shirt buttons, and felt his chest. It was bloody, coagulated blood, and cold. I was sure he was dead.' Jack shrugged. 'Then I waited for the police and the emergency services.'

'You have omitted something, I believe, Mr Bell.'

He thought for a second. 'Oh yes, I went to get my telescope.'

'Why was that?'

'The man was dead. So I could be no help to him, and I didn't want to leave 600 quid's worth of telescope on its own.'

'You put it in a wheelbarrow, I believe.'

'Yes. I'm a builder. I keep a wheelbarrow in my van. It's not the most portable of scopes, but OK in a barrow. I got back just before you arrived.'

'Where was your van?'

'On Capel Road where I had parked it, about 100 yards away.'

'Can you tell us why there is blood in your van?'

A hand went onto Jack's knee. The solicitor's warning. He hardly needed it, it hit him like a slap round the face. Blood in his van. How could that be? When he'd loaded up his telescope outside his house, it had been dark. He hadn't noted any blood, but he'd been obsessed with Nova and their row.

'I didn't know there was any,' he said.

DI Hawley smiled, a superior smile that had all the answers. 'I put it to you, Mr Bell, that you carried the body in your van to the Flats. You unloaded it, most likely into your wheelbarrow, where we also found traces of blood, and ferried it to the site where you said you accidentally found it.'

'The body was never in my van. I didn't ferry it anywhere.'

'Can you account for the blood?'

'Quite obviously someone put it there. And it wasn't me. I keep all sorts of tools in my van. It's open much of the time when I'm working. Someone put it there to frame me. How much blood was there?'

'I am asking the questions, Mr Bell.'

Obviously someone had planted it while Jack was working in Tom Litt's back garden. So this was their ace. Blood in his van, his wheelbarrow too. No wonder she looked so smug.

Why had he missed it? There couldn't have been much, or even with his head all over the shop, he'd have seen it.

'When did you last see Mr Litt, the victim?'

'I didn't see him yesterday at all. The day before, I saw him a couple of times. I asked him about payment. He told me to send an invoice.'

'How much are you owed?'

'About £800.'

'Are you short of money?'

'Yes. Things are tight. So why kill the man who's about to pay me? He can't now.'

He felt he'd scored a goal, though Hawley was four up with ten minutes to play. Her kick off.

'The cry you heard on the Flats. What were the words?'

'Help me, help me! A few times.'

'I suggest that is pure fabrication, Mr Bell. There was no cry.'

'I distinctly heard a cry. It must have been to draw me over. Part of the frame-up.'

'No cry. And there was no running man.'

'There was someone running, not necessarily a man.'

'You are clutching at straws, Mr Bell.' She turned to her colleague. 'Would you take over the interview, DC Alagia?'

The detective constable nodded. He glanced down at his notes.

'What was your relationship with Mrs Litt?' he said.

Jack shrugged. New tack. What were they going to throw at him now?

Stay cool.

'She was the wife of my client. She made me the odd cup of tea. I would knock on the kitchen door and ask to use the toilet.'

'How often did you see her?'

'Every day. She was at home, Mr Litt was at work. I caught him in the morning first thing, occasionally during the day. But she was there most of the time.'

'When was your last time with her?'

'Yesterday afternoon. About three. I was bricklaying, building a wall at the end of their patio. We talked about how the job was going. The sky was quite clear, I said I might go over the Flats with the telescope in the evening.'

'She said the last time she spoke to you, you were in bed with her.'

Another slammer. He sat back in his seat, his head working overtime. This is why Hawley is so confident. He could see it adding up. All against him: blood in the van, screwing the client's wife, the coincidence of him finding the corpse...

'She's lying,' he said.

'She says you had been having an affair for several weeks.'

'Absolute rubbish.'

'She was home all day, you were there too...'

'Bricklaying. Count the bricks, the courses I put in.'

He knew, as he said it, this wasn't a strong argument as he was a slow bricklayer. Time for an affair? He could see them with their calculators, bringing in a bricklayer as an expert witness, working out that he could have spent two hours in bed with the wife and still laid the bricks.

It was adding up. Blood, affair, they didn't believe the cry or the running man. His story was a frame-up, theirs far simpler: Jack was the killer.

'She says that you seduced her.'

He shook his head.

'More lies.' He slapped his hands to his head. 'I never once touched her. Always called her Mrs Litt.' A sudden thought. 'She knew I might be on the Flats. It's a frame up, can't you see? I was the fall guy.'

'She said that you and she went to bed most days.'

Stone spoke up for the first time. 'My client denies this. He has said three times there was no affair.'

'She says there was,' said Alagia.

'And he has said clearly, there wasn't.'

'It depends who you believe,' broke in DI Hawley.

'So it does,' said Stone. 'Can we move on?'

'I have a point,' said Jack. He had been thinking furiously.

'I haven't asked you anything,' said Alagia.

'You have,' retorted Jack. 'Repeatedly. You have said I was having an affair with Mrs Litt.'

'And you have said, in spite of her saying you were, that you were not.'

'She said we went to the bedroom most days.'

DI Hawley interrupted. 'We have dealt with this, Mr Bell. As your solicitor says, we should move on.'

'I have never been in her bedroom. Not once.'

'Let's move on, please. Control your client, Mr Stone.'

'You won't find a single hair or fingerprint of mine in that bedroom.'

Surely he'd scored another goal. But boy, did he have to fight for it. She was doing her best to shut him down. She had her case and didn't want him adding an iota of doubt.

'This concludes our interview,' she said.

'You are not listening to me,' protested Jack.

'It's all on record.' She indicated the tape recorder.

'My client wants to know,' said Stone, 'whether the Litt bedroom is going to be examined forensically.'

'If necessary.'

'It is necessary!' yelled Jack. 'I am innocent!'

He stood up, leaning forward, his head almost against Hawley's.

'There was no affair! And examining the bedroom will prove it, even to you!'

She grimaced, wiping a fleck of spit off her face.

Helplessness and hopelessness ran through him. He was going to be stitched up and locked away forever. Jack drew back his fist. And in an instant, Alagia was on him. He knew at once it was stupidity, caught on camera. Alagia twisted him round into a half nelson. Jack struggled, other cops rushed into the room.

'It's a set-up! Can't you see!' he yelled as he struggled.

Jack was forced to the floor on his back and snapped into handcuffs.

Chapter 8

He was in the cell, seated on the bench, back and shoulders aching after the struggle with the cops, head sunk into his hands.

Peter Stone was standing above him. There was a policeman standing by the open door of the cell. Stone had been asked whether he felt safe in Jack's presence.

'It's not me he's accusing,' he'd said.

Stone put a hand on Jack's shoulder.

'Oh, Mr Bell, you were making some good points, until your outburst.'

Jack grimaced and looked up at the solicitor, who was like a kindly uncle. He felt he'd let him down.

'She wasn't listening,' he said.

'That doesn't matter,' said Stone. 'It's recorded on video and tape. A jury will hear it. But now...' he threw out his arms, 'you have shown them you are a man with a violent temper.'

'Likely to murder.'

'That's what the prosecution will suggest.'

Jack shook his head. He was weary of himself. A second of stupidity. That's all. Half a punch, it never even arrived before they were on him. No more than ten minutes ago. Reverse the film, take out the punch. A director's cut, showing him to be a mature, sensible fellow.

'I saw red. They had concocted a case,' he said, 'to send me to jail for 20 years.'

'You must not assist the prosecution, Mr Bell. Imagine a jury member seeing that bit of video. You, about to hit an inspector, then fighting with other officers as they incapacitate you and put you in handcuffs. What would you think when you saw this violent man?'

'Not good thoughts.'

Jack could imagine it, the prosecutor showing the bit of video as often as he could get away with. A woman in the jury box shuddering. Violence in a police station! The defendant must be a hardened criminal, guilty as charged, and the longer he is locked up the safer for the rest of us.

Too late for regrets. It was done. Caught on video. He must be a model prisoner from now on.

'Do you think I'm guilty?' he said.

'I honestly don't know,' said Stone. 'I can't see why you'd kill him, unless you were having an affair with his wife.'

'Utter rubbish.'

'But throwing a punch...' Stone lifted his fist as if to demonstrate. 'You could hardly have done anything worse.'

'I felt doomed. Fitted up. They kept coming up with stuff. The blood in my van, I know nothing about it. An affair going on for weeks. This is such a stitch up, and that cop is going to hammer me with it, never mind the truth.'

He stopped, there was no judge or jury here, just an old kindly solicitor and a stony faced cop at the door who would believe his fellow cops, and not Jack.

'I reacted like a teenager,' he said.

'I'm afraid there's little I can do, Mr Bell. I am simply the duty solicitor. You must help yourself. There will be further interviews, no doubt. They'll get nasty, they want to provoke you, to make you react. It's a game, but it is one you have to decide not to play. No striking out, please, no matter what they say. Violence makes their case for them.'

'Stupidity is my middle name. But I assure you that Mrs Litt is a bare-faced liar. I said to the cop, examine the bedroom. And it was clear she wouldn't. It didn't fit her story.'

Jack was incensed, reliving those last minutes in the interview room. That feeling of helplessness, of being strung up.

'Mr Bell, if they do not check the bedroom for your DNA and fingerprints, that will show them as sloppy. A good barrister will hammer that hard when DI Hawley goes on the stand. And what can her answer be?'

'She'll try to brush it off.'

'That will show her to be prejudiced, to have a one track mind.'

He could see that. There must be other holes in this case. She had a tale, but he had one too. Things were looking bad, but he mustn't make it worse.

'I was daft enough to believe they'd realise their mistakes,' he said with a wry smile, 'and they'd let me go this morning with an apology.' He turned to Stone in a weak appeal. 'Is this definitely going to court?'

'I can't see otherwise, Mr Bell. First step is the magistrate's court, probably tomorrow. It will be a formality. You will plead not guilty, I assume?'

'I will.'

'It's a serious case, murder. Too serious for a magistrate's court. Once you plead not guilty, you will be remanded in custody until your trial comes up at crown court.'

'How long will that be?'

'The way things are going, Mr Bell, who knows? Six months, nine months, a year... The whole system is in chaos.'

Chapter 9

Jack paced back and forth, from door to back wall, swinging his arms to prove he still had some life in him, from back wall to door. Four paces and then a short one. He adjusted his paces, so they would fit exactly. Five paces.

It passed the time.

At least he knew what they had on him. That was hardly counting his blessings. He had to prepare for further surprises. Stuck in here, what could he do to prove his innocence? No phone, and the duty solicitor gone.

He needed outside help.

A little later, two policemen brought him a sandwich and tea. They came in warily, having registered him as a dangerous criminal, ordering him to the back of the cell. He did as he was bid, and they quickly put the food on the bench and left.

Jack called after them, 'Thank you.'

He had to practise his manners. From now on, no hostility. Or at least don't show it. It would take time enough to wash away his big scene. A reputation, he didn't need. He'd have to find religion or some other salvation to show he had forsworn violence. Maybe after ten years inside, sewing mailbags, no, they wouldn't do that any more, stitching shoes then, one warden might say to another, don't worry about Jack, he's calmed down the last few years. He might even become a trustie, and help out in the kitchen or the library.

Perhaps in five years, he could go to the governor and ask to set up an astronomy group. A surprising request which the governor would look at suspiciously. Too risky to allow prisoners in the yard in the dark. Might be just a ruse for an escape attempt. Or they'd let him in the yard, but wash out the night sky in floodlights, which would make any viewing useless.

Would Mia come and visit him? For how long? She'd have to bite her tongue at school, at college. She couldn't say my dad's inside for murder. Easier to push him out of her mind for a while.

As for Nova, she was a cop. Cops keep away from murderers. Don't have them as lovers. Or even friends.

How would he survive a life sentence? All he knew was a construct of prison movies he'd seen. Screws who beat you up, prisoners who did you over in the shower for some imagined slight, riots with prisoners barricading themselves in, and screaming insults from the rooftops.

It was difficult to think of the alternative. To imagine himself walking out of the police station, free, the cops admitting their mistakes.

Like they always did, of course.

The trial, a jury, a judge, a prosecutor in a wig... He stopped.

They hadn't proved the blood to be Tom Litt's. But who else could it be from? If he was being set up, it had to be Litt's. And what else could this be, other than a frame up? From the cry on the Flats, to the blood, to Mrs Litt and the affair. What else might they yet get on him?

More lying witnesses?

All it needed was the weapon to be found in his flat. The same gun as used for half a dozen other murders, and he'd never walk free. They had the keys to his flat, and so were free to plant whatever necessary to tie him up like a trussed chicken.

Having made himself thoroughly miserable, Jack examined the sandwich, cheese and pickle. He wasn't hungry but nibbled at it. He must eat, if just to keep his mind clear. The tea was tepid, wet and sweet. He wouldn't complain on TripAdvisor.

There must be a way through. It was these walls, so confining, so depressing. Hardly conducive to thinking straight. Not even a window. How could hope not dwindle?

He thought about Mrs Litt. What was her first name? Yvonne, though he'd never used it. They might ask him if he found her attractive. As it happened, he did, but that would be the wrong answer. Every question a trick question, he had to assume a jury was listening in. Any answer was for them, not for the cops.

'She wasn't my sort,' he might say.

Would he have been up for it? The right answer is No. But in reality, an attractive woman, her husband at work... Still has to be No. His client's wife. Give himself a break, he had some control. Besides, there was Nova. He was in a relationship, or had been till last night. So it was no, no, never, Mrs Robinson.

Mrs Litt would be a witness, of course. The victim's widow, so there'd be plenty of sympathy for the poor woman. But rather muddled, as she was having an affair with the murderer. What might she wear in the box? Black would make her a hypocrite, and bright colours a wicked woman. She would be advised by the prosecution to keep her clothing subdued.

To lay it on the foul builder.

He was already thinking in terms of the court case. Mrs Litt in the witness box, sworn in to tell the truth and nothing but the truth. Pure tabloid fodder. He would be famous for a week. How might that work out in jail? Get him praise or get him beaten up in the shower?

He wanted to stop this thinking in circles. There was too little to go on. The trial could be six months or a year away. How to survive that time.

Jigsaw puzzles, crosswords. It's why jails are full of drugs. Men without hope, passing time, somehow or other.

Dare he think of getting off? How?

Mrs Litt was the key. There were only two options to her testimony. She was lying, but either freely or because she was forced to do it. If the former, then she was the murderer, or in league with the murderer, while framing Jack. He couldn't see her doing the deed. She was quite slight, too slight to move a body, so would need a hit man, or maybe a lover.

Find the lover.

The alternative was, she'd been forced to drop Jack in it. This was so complicated, so befuddled in unknowns. Who, why, what? Someone who had threatened her and forced her to lie, in order to set Jack up as the patsy. Her husband must have been up to something, crossed someone, to get himself murdered.

Both scenarios had no scintilla of evidence. And he couldn't get any, stuck in here. Damn you, Mrs Litt. She was the crux of any defence he must build.

Why was she lying?

The cell door opened. Jack had reached the far wall in his to-ing and fro-ing. A tall cop stood there in a white shirt and navy trousers, beside him was Nova.

'You'll be OK with him, Nova?'

'I'll be OK,' she said. 'I know him.'

'I'll leave the door open in case,' he said with a smile. And left.

She was in a navy blue dress suit, a white blouse, brown flat shoes. Well, she was Fayyad's sidekick, and he insisted on smartness. Her blonde hair was neat, tied back in a ponytail, just a hint of make-up. She was short, quite stocky, but not fat. A good footballer with the Met first team, but playing less now she was a detective with irregular hours.

Jack came to greet her.

'Sit down,' she hissed. Her hands out, signalling him to stay back.

He sat obediently on the bench. She took the one chair and sat on it, out of touching distance.

'No hugging, no familiarity,' she said. 'They are watching.' She pointed up at the camera. 'I'm here to ask you questions about Wanstead Flats and your telescope

40

outings. I told them your nightly visits to the Flats might involve drugs.'

'What!' Jack threw his arms up. 'You mean murder is not enough?'

'Don't panic. It's just what I told them to get in. I know you are not a killer. But I work here, Jack. Your case is nothing to do with me as a cop. I can't just drop in and see my lover whenever I wish.'

'I get that,' he said. 'Thanks for coming.'

He wanted to hug her, get some warmth, but saw her dilemma. She was on his side, she was on their side too. But she was here, like an angel dropped from heaven.

Prepare for shocks.

Nova took a notebook out of her pocket.

'Must make it look like I'm here on business.'

'I'm in shtuck,' he said.

'Don't I know it. It's all over the station: the bloke accused of murder tried to clock DI Hawley.'

'Dumbest thing I ever did.'

'And you've done some pretty dumb things, Jack my lad.'

'I can't argue with that. Do you know about my case?'

She nodded. 'I looked you up on Holmes. You are accused of murdering Tom Litt. There's blood in your van, and his wife said that you and she were in a relationship.' She stopped and looked Jack square in the eye. 'I know you are not a murderer, but were you shagging the victim's wife?'

'No.'

'Is that the total truth? I know you guys, given half a chance.'

'I never once touched her.'

'You sure, you absolutely sure, one hundred per cent, that you never ever got into bed with her?'

'Yes.'

'Then why did she say you did?'

Jack slapped his hands.

'That's it, the nub of it, Nova. That's what I have to find out. Fayyad has trained you well.'

'Fayyad wanted to come and see you, but he can't. As an inspector, he mustn't interfere with another inspector's case. Protocol. So he and I made up a tale so I could come.' She glanced at her empty notebook. 'Better write something down.'

She wrote a few rapid lines.

'All these cells have cameras,' she said as she wrote, 'in case of suicide, that sort of thing. So we are on view.'

'No hugging.'

'I'm sorry about our row,' she said. 'I regretted it soon after. My fault for once. I was going to make it up to you.'

'You have. By coming. This place is awful. You feel guilty just being here. Everyone has got me down as the killer. Look at these shapeless clothes. They stripped me naked. I haven't got a thing to my name.'

'Mia phoned me a couple of hours ago. Told me you had been arrested. Quite an organiser, your daughter. She's fixed a meeting tonight with herself, me and her mother, at her mum's place. Operation Jack Bell.'

A spark of hope in a dark tunnel.

He said, 'Tell 'em I'm OK. I'm not, but say I am.'

'You'll be going to magistrate's court in the morning. Murder is way too serious for a lower court, so they'll pass you on to crown court. And while awaiting trial, you'll be remanded in custody.'

'What does that mean?'

'You'll be taken to a prison, not here any more. But as a remand prisoner, you can wear your own clothes and get more visitors. Can't do educational stuff though.'

'Just stew till the case comes up.'

The high of her visit was draining away at the thought of the months and months while they built up the case against him. And he dealt with violent prisoners, screws, and the deadening routine.

'You mustn't hit cops, Jack.'

'You should have told me that yesterday.'

'I didn't think it needed saying.' She shook her fists. 'I want to shake you, and hug you. Which one first?' She scrawled a few words in her book. 'Neither, I'm afraid. Back to business, Mr Bell. Your ex, Mia's mum... Keep forgetting her name.'

'Alison.'

'Alison. Mustn't forget. She is going to bring you some clothing and stuff this afternoon. I can't do that, or I would have brought them now. What would you like her to bring?'

'A phone.'

'That's out. What else?'

'Notebook, pens, proper clothing, Mia's got a key to my flat.' He was grasping for what he wanted. 'Chocolate, fruit, books, magazines, toothbrush, my electric razor... Can I have all that?'

'Sure, sure. You are not convicted. Innocent until proven guilty.'

'Wish they believed that.'

'You haven't been to trial, and that gives you some privileges while in custody. Proper jail, not this holding nick, there you get a prison account, we'll put some money in it so you can buy stuff at the prison shop. Get a phone card. Alison is going to get you a solicitor, one I recommended. She's good, the solicitor that is, can't vouch for your ex.' She glanced at her watch. 'And that's about it for now. I'm going to have to leave you, I'm afraid. Sorry it's so brief.'

'I wish I could kiss you.'

'Ditto. But we can't. I'm a cop, and you are on a murder charge. I know you didn't do it, and I'd love to throw my arms around you, but not in my home cop shop.'

'I love you.'

She laughed, throwing her arms up.

'First time you've ever said that, Jack. Do you have to be on a murder charge to come out with it? Three words. Not so hard, were they?'

'I so wanted to see you.'

'I did all I could to get here, so maybe I love you too.'

'Maybe?'

'I'm not on a murder rap, so I don't have to admit anything.'

'You could lie. Everyone else seems to be doing it.'

They gazed into each other's eyes, the air between them magnetised, attempting to draw them together, fighting the need to be seen as separate poles.

'Got to leave you, love. I know it's horrible here, and it's going to get worse before it gets better. But me, Mia and Alison are having our pow-wow tonight. We know you are innocent, and we will get you out one way or another.'

He had to believe her. There were people on his side. He wasn't alone, no matter how it felt in these bare walls. Three women were rooting for him, though there was one who wasn't.

'What do you know about DI Hawley?' he said.

'Kate Hawley is an ambitious cow. She gets results one way or another.'

'I've seen how. She dismisses anything that doesn't fit.'

'That's how you get promoted, dearest. Get a result. Fayyad doesn't like her, she's too full of herself.' Nova threw up her hands in exasperation. 'I can't be here passing on station gossip.' She rose. 'I love you too, Jack Bell. Chin up, we're on your case, mate.'

And with a wave, she was away.

Chapter 10

Nova's visit had cheered him up. He wasn't like a medieval prisoner thrown into the oubliette, shackled, forgotten, left to starve. He had people on the outside rooting for him. The evidence against him was stark, but with visits he could get inconsistencies checked out. Look for holes in Hawley's tale.

Before Nova's visit, they'd given him a menu to tick off for lunch. He'd been surprised to be given a choice, as he thought it was take it or leave it. From their own canteen, he'd been told. Jack had quickly ticked a few items, hardly caring, as choice in food was low on his list. Choice in detective? How about that?

Two cops came with the lunch tray, ordering the dangerous prisoner back against the far wall. They ventured in, put the food on the bench and left hurriedly. He called thank you, knowing he'd need a thousand of those to leave any impression.

He'd forgotten what he'd chosen. Burger and chips with a little salad, that'd do. Tasty, though the chips were a little cold, and not up to a type 2 diabetic diet, which said cut out the fried food and eat more fruit and veg. But he got what he'd carelessly ordered. Not that he'd be here long.

A prison cell was being made ready.

The sweet was a strawberry yogurt, plus the customary sweet tea. No knives, just a plastic fork and spoon, in case he might stab someone. Or himself. He ate slowly, he had time to play with, to pass somehow.

Nova had said she loved him, sort of. It was said as a goodbye, so don't count on it. Realistically, the relationship would die if he was locked up for months. Even on remand,

45

awaiting trial, he'd be inside for a year. And if he lost his case, murder would get him a 20 years plus sentence. He would serve that well and truly alone.

Jack let his food digest for what he judged to be 30 minutes, and was considering doing some exercises: push ups, stretches, arm flings. He could make a little routine, when the door opened.

There stood a tall, male cop, his hair short and almost white, his face pale pink, wearing the customary white shirt and navy blue trousers. He was holding a carrier bag.

'Special delivery for Jack Bell.'

He held up the bag and came into the cell. Either not afraid of the dangerous inmate, or a 4th Dan in some deadly martial art.

'Who is it from?'

'A young lady with lots of frizzy chestnut hair. There's a note inside.' He caught Jack's reproach. 'Anything that comes in for an inmate has to be inspected. No phones, drugs or weapons. It's all got to be kosher.'

Jack nodded. Prison was prison. They ticked and checked and watched; some things you just had to accept. It would take a Home Secretary's ruling to change them. He took the carrier bag, curious as to the contents.

He began laying out the contents beside him on the bench. There was an opened envelope inside with Jack Bell written on it, in Mia's handwriting. Good for her. He'd read it when the officer had gone.

'I hear you punched DI Hawley.'

Jack smiled. 'Is that how it's going around? I swung a punch but it didn't arrive.'

'Pity.'

Jack looked up at the young cop in surprise. Hawley obviously wasn't popular.

'I got jumped on by an army of cops,' he said. 'And now everyone is treating me like a man-eating tiger.'

46

'You can't hit a cop,' said the officer, 'not even Hawley. Though the sooner she gets promotion, the sooner she's out of my way.'

'Wish she was out of mine.'

The cop smiled. 'Don't let her rile you. It all goes on your record and that will follow you wherever they send you.'

'I thought, she's going to get me, no matter what.'

'I'll leave you with your goody bag.'

He picked up the lunch tray and left.

'Thank you,' Jack called after him.

He had enough warnings on Hawley. It sort of amazed him, and yet it didn't. She wanted a result, at any cost. No matter that it sent him down for 20 years. If in 15 years, it was shown to be a miscarriage of justice, she'd have been promoted beyond caring.

One step at a time. Thinking of a long stretch would just crush any effort he could make now. Think what he could do now.

The contents of the bag were laid out. Mia's pick. Toothpaste and brush, electric shaver, comb, socks, a pair of trainers, a Daily Mirror, his astronomy mag, a notebook and pen, and a KitKat.

Oh, good girl!

Jack threw the flip flops into a corner and put on his socks and trainers. He stood up, to feel them on the ground. Much better. He walked a few steps in them, as if he were telling Hawley, here I stand.

Utter crap, but it lifted him for a minute or two. He opened the KitKat and ate the chocolate fingers one by one, savouring the sweetness, as he read Mia's note. She didn't handwrite much, and it showed in her just-decipherable message.

Dear Dad

Nova phoned me. She said you had nothing in your cell, so could I get you some things. She told me what I could take. I've changed my mind about her, she's a cop but she's OK. Me, Mum

47

and her are having a meeting tonight to talk about the best way of helping you. I didn't go to the demo or to school. I was too upset by you being arrested. Anyway, it wouldn't do for me to get arrested too. The charge is ridiculous. If that woman detective had any sense she could see it's all a frame up. But lots of cops are stupid, some are bastards, and some are both. Not Nova, she's the exception that proves the rule. Mum is coming to see you after school with some clothes.

Lots of love
Mia xxx

Chapter 11

Jack read the Daily Mirror Mia had brought him. The news seemed superficial compared to his own tale. Wars, affairs of film stars, sport, even famine shrank to insignificance. Though the story of child cruelty held him. A four year old boy had been killed by his stepfather. His body was covered in bruises, while for over a year social workers had been fobbed off by the parents as the kid endured endless misery in his short life.

It made Jack angry, which was senseless, as he couldn't do anything. But it hurt that a man could be so cruel. A male member of the human race, white, British, close to his own age, so many traits that fitted him too.

He might meet him inside.

Jack did half the crossword before he lost interest. 'US author died 1888, Louisa May .....' Mia would know, he didn't care, and tossed the paper aside. He flipped through his astronomy mag. The stars would still be there when he came out. More his realm. There'd be some slight change if he got a long stretch, but nothing he'd notice, not in a human lifetime. Precession, they called it, when in a few thousand years, the pole star would no longer be what we now call Polaris. Due to the slow wobble of the earth's axis. The constellations would change too, as the stars in them weren't related, just seemed to be from our viewpoint. And when the viewpoint changed, so did the stars in relation to one another.

The police had his telescope. He hoped they weren't messing up the alignment. Not that they'd care or compensate him. He could bear with it if they didn't break the mirror or the eyepiece. In an evening, most likely, he could re-set it.

Jack took a stroll for what might have been five minutes or longer. To and fro, swinging his arms, wall to door, in his newly arrived trainers. His feet at least felt free. Now he must work on the rest of his body.

They came for him as he was reading an article on exo-planets.

Jack was handcuffed and led to the interview room. He was left there with the duty solicitor and a cop who stood at the back. The solicitor was not Peter Stone, who no doubt had other work to do. This one was a middle aged woman, on the plump side, in a grey dress suit. She was lightly made up apart from lipstick, purple and too prominent. Distracting. It made him think of the oddity of painting lips at all, when presumably it was meant to make her more attractive.

'Mary Lee,' she said.

'Jack Bell,' he replied.

'Sorry about him,' she said indicating the cop, 'but you have a reputation. You were fighting with five officers.'

'I threw a punch in a fit of madness,' he said, wondering how many times he'd have to offer his excuses. 'One came at me, then the others jumped in. I was just trying to stop them hitting me.'

'That's not what they say.'

'Cops stick together,' he said, aware he sounded like Mia. 'I threw a punch. It didn't get anywhere, and the rest was me trying to protect myself as they took revenge.' He held up his handcuffed hands. 'I come in peace.'

She smiled. 'Good. Let's get to business. They want you to confess, Mr Bell. My advice is don't. I don't care whether you are guilty or not.' She held up a hand. 'Don't try to convince me one way or the other, I am not the jury. If you ever feel like confessing, talk to your solicitor first. You are getting one?'

'It's being arranged. And I'm innocent.'

50

She smiled. He liked her in spite of the lipstick, but was in no position to give cosmetics advice.

'I shall believe you, for now at least,' she said. 'Not that my opinion makes the slightest difference. I think we are all but ready. Think before you answer anything. No hitting anyone, please.'

'I have learnt my lesson.' He stifled a yawn at another admonishment.

'I'm glad of that, Mr Bell.' She paused an instant. 'I have two signals as the interview progresses. If I step on your foot, it means you don't have to answer. If I squeeze your arm, it means we should confer privately. Any questions?'

He had none.

'Let's get on with it.'

Chapter 12

Four people were at the table. Jack with Mary Lee at his side, and DI Hawley with DC Alagia opposite them. The tape and video were running, Hawley had given date and time and named those present. Two cops were at the back wall, added security he surmised, with truncheons in their belt. As if they were daring him to try something.

Any excuse and they'd crack his head like a hard boiled egg.

Mary Lee suggested that Jack's handcuffs should be removed, a suggestion denied by DI Hawley. Jack might be more comfortable with them removed, Hawley said, but she would be more comfortable with them left on.

Hawley had had her hair cut, and was wearing a little more make-up. He could smell her perfume. A little cloying in this closed room. He guessed she was going out after she'd done with him. Alagia was stony-faced. He'd had the speed of a rattlesnake when stopping Jack's punch. This interview, Jack would be the model prisoner, knowing exactly how it would go if he were to try anything. Handcuffed, four cops in the room, including the two against the back wall, he'd be crackers to raise a fingernail to Hawley, unless he'd given up on freedom.

The interview proceeded.

'The blood in your van, Mr Bell,' said Hawley, 'has gone for DNA analysis. But at this stage we know it's the same blood group as the victim's. I'd be surprised if the DNA is not proved to be his.'

Jack shrugged. He'd be surprised too. The frame-up demanded it.

'Would you like to tell us how the blood got there?'

'I've told you. Someone put it there. But it wasn't me.'

Hawley was looking at him keenly, a slight smirk on her face as if she knew something he didn't. Very likely, considering she was the investigating officer and he'd been doing the Daily Mirror crossword.

'Blood in your van, your affair with Mrs Litt...'

'There was no affair. She's a liar.'

She went on as if he hadn't spoken. 'The victim being your employer Tom Litt, and the coincidence of you finding him.' Her fingers wiggled to indicate quotes on 'finding him'. 'And the tale of a cry from a man who'd been dead for hours...'

'Have you a question, DI Hawley?' said Mary Lee.

'I was wondering, with so much damning evidence, if Mr Bell might choose to confess.'

Jack felt a foot pressed on his. It wasn't necessary.

'I am not guilty,' he said.

'Consider, Mr Bell, the publicity of the court case, the affair with your employer's wife, the murder of your client... Consider how it will affect your family. Your daughter especially.'

A foot went onto his. He could feel himself colouring up. Her tactic was obviously to make him angry, so he would come out with something damning.

'I am innocent,' he said through a squeezed throat.

He picked up the plastic cup in front of him, saw Hawley flinch, as if he was going to throw it at her, and Alagia at the ready. He sensed movement from the cops at the back. He imagined them gripping their truncheons, aching to hit him.

Too predictable how the scene would run, if he were so cavalier. Handcuffed hands around the cup, he drew it to his lips and slowly sipped. A dribble ran down his chin. Mary Lee wiped it off with a tissue.

'Thank you,' he said, grateful for a little humanity. He put down the cup. 'I am innocent,' he said, 'as I have told you repeatedly. And I am offended by that cheap jibe against my daughter.'

'Court cases are harrowing,' said Hawley, 'and with press intrusion, devastating for members of the family.'

'I am not going to confess to something I didn't do to further your career.'

Alagia smiled, obviously appreciating the hit against his boss. Jack wondered how they got on. He couldn't imagine she'd be easy to work with. Bossy, impatient, too certain of things.

DI Hawley held up a plastic bag. Inside was a cufflink with a lion imprint, blood stained.

'Do you recognise this?'

He looked closely, guessing what she was going to say next.

'No.'

'It was found in your van. Mrs Litt has identified it as belonging to her husband. When a body is moved, things get dislodged. Small things, like cufflinks. Imagine this item being passed round the jury.'

'Someone set me up,' he said. 'The cufflink came with the blood. You are stuck on that one scenario.'

'Because it is so obviously the truth. You aren't being held for no reason, Mr Bell. The evidence against you is compelling and building up. A confession may lessen your sentence, but would also lessen media intrusion on Mrs Litt and your family.'

He pressed his cuffed hands under the table, so he wouldn't be tempted to strike out, as futile and stupid as it might be.

'How many times do I have to tell you I am innocent?' he said.

Mary Lee said, 'Unless you have anything else, DI Hawley, I think we can call a halt to this interview.'

Hawley ignored her interjection.

'You have been going out with DC Taylor.'

Nova. That had to come up. How could it not? It wasn't a secret relationship.

'Yes,' he said, 'though she was frequently too busy.'

'So busy, you had plenty of time for a relationship with Mrs Litt.'

'I never had a relationship with Mrs Litt. She is lying.'

'When was the last time you went out with DC Taylor?'

He thought back. The last time.

'Four days ago. Though last night, we'd planned a date at Stratford Picturehouse. But she didn't show.'

If only she had. He wouldn't have gone on the Flats with his telescope, found the body, phoned the cops...

'I suggest you knew she wouldn't come.'

This was a little tortuous. He wasn't following her reasoning.

'She was an alibi, Mr Bell. You knew she was busy on a case. And you had a body to dispose of.'

Jack laughed.

'This is so ridiculous. You twist everything to fit your absurd tale.'

'It is your denial which is absurd, Mr Bell. The evidence is building up and when the blood is proved to be from the victim, the case against you will be watertight. I leave you to consider making a confession. For the sake of your loved ones, if for no one else.'

Chapter 13

Jack had a short post-interview meeting with Mary Lee. She said his restraint had been good. Hawley had been out to get him angry, and he hadn't taken the bait. Tomorrow morning, she told him, he'd be going to magistrate's court. Just a formality, as all cases went there to begin with. But he would be tried, as with all serious cases, in crown court.

Once that was dealt with, he'd be taken to a prison. She couldn't say where.

He thanked her, and was taken back to the cell, the handcuffs removed. He reflected on the interview. No major surprises and he hadn't hit anyone. A cufflink. Whoever planted the blood planted that. And they were exaggerating his capacity for violence. It would be used in evidence against him, be sure of that. Video snippets of him in handcuffs would add to the impression of a dangerous prisoner. Someone a jury would be remiss to let back out on the streets.

They sapped him of energy, the interviews, the piled on evidence. He had to be absolutely alert, knowing a wrong word, an innocent mistake, and it would be on the record. It was a game. No wonder experienced cons simply said, 'No comment' to any question. It might make you look shifty, but it gave nothing away and made for boring viewing, with little to show a jury.

He couldn't just 'No comment'. He needed to talk back to the cops. Pick holes in their case. He must sow some doubt in their fixed tale. Though, he had no sign it had worked at all up to now. These case hardened cops had heard everything, knew every excuse in the book, all the lies, all the cries of innocence. They believed him guilty and would do all in their power to prove it.

'Stand back!' came a call through the spy hole.

He went to the rear of the cell, as a tray of tea and biscuits was brought in by a male and a female officer, and left on the bench.

He thanked them.

'All part of the service, sir,' said the woman as she left.

He was seeing a lot of different coppers. Maybe they were curious to see the murderer. Or it was just shift patterns. A busy place, the station. A costly place to stay at. Locking him up, feeding him, questioning him, transporting him, didn't come cheap, and they must have other things to do.

One mustn't imagine he was the only criminal locked up here. He'd heard cell doors closing and the odd voices in the outside corridor, though he hadn't seen any other prisoners. Likely he was the only murderer. He corrected himself: accused murderer. He was innocent until proved guilty. Hawley wanted him to confess. To make her life easier. Push her up the ladder.

He had drunk half the tea and had a mouth full of biscuit when the tall policeman entered.

'You have a visitor, sir. In the custody suite. Cuffs on, I'm afraid.'

Jack put his hands out, knowing it was pointless to argue. Their bat, their ball, their whistle.

Handcuffed, he was led out of the cell, along the corridor, to the custody suite. Sitting on the sofa was Alison, his ex, Mia's mother. She had a small suitcase by her.

'Must Jack wear those?' she said indicating the handcuffs.

'I am afraid so, madam. He tried to hit an officer.'

Jack kept out of it. Nothing he said would help.

'I assure you he won't hit me,' said Alison. 'We were married ten years, had plenty of rows, but he never once laid a hand on me. I'll say that for him.'

A minimal character witness, Jack thought.

'Orders,' said the officer with a shrug. 'If you don't like him in cuffs, I shall have to return him to his cell.'

'It's OK, Alison,' said Jack. 'I'm getting used to them.'

'Then I'll have to accept, and talk to you while you are handcuffed,' she said, 'but I am not happy.'

The officer didn't reply.

Jack sat at the other end of the sofa. The officer sat on a chair by the door.

Alison was smartly dressed in a green check dress-suit, efficient flat shoes on her feet. Should she be minded to, she could run for a bus or climb a ladder. Neither very likely for a school principal. Her chestnut hair was neatly cut, reaching her shoulders. The same colour as their daughter's far bushier growth. Mother and daughter were the same size and build but opposed in tidiness.

'Have you patched things up with Mia?' he said.

She flapped a dismissive hand. 'Forgotten. There's more important things on the agenda.' She looked to the officer. 'Can I hand over the suitcase?'

He nodded. 'It's been gone through, madam.'

'Clothes and a few things I picked up for you,' said Alison to Jack. 'And Nova said earplugs might be useful.'

'Thanks for the clothes,' he said, rifling through the clothing. 'I hate this baggy gear.' He pulled at the weak elastic waist band to demonstrate. 'One size fits all.'

'How are they treating you?'

'They've only beaten me up once,' he said with a half laugh. 'Though it was my fault. And don't they keep telling me.'

Alison shook her head at his admission. She was quite beautiful in a somewhat forbidding way. Her school was rated excellent. When they had married, she had been a class teacher. Seven years ago, she'd kicked him out for drunkenness. Thoroughly deserved, he would admit. And she'd risen up the ranks, divorcing him along the way.

He had loved her once. Now their relationship was more complicated. Sometimes they got on, sometimes he resented her. Partly a class thing. She was an ambitious school principal, he a builder. Their only glue, a daughter in common. Without Mia, they would never see each other.

'Mia tried explaining the case to me,' she said, 'but it doesn't make sense.' She peered at him closely. 'You are not a murderer, Jack. Never, ever.'

'The nicest thing you've said in ages.'

He smiled and she returned it.

'I've got you a solicitor,' she said.

'I'll pay you back.'

She held up a hand. 'Please don't talk money. I can afford it. They are putting me in charge of a four-school academy.' She chuckled. 'I didn't mention my eco-warrior daughter at the interview, and fortunately my ex hadn't yet been charged with murder.'

'I wouldn't want to hold you back.'

She grimaced.

'You are innocent, anyone with any sense could see that.'

'Would you be a character witness? In court.'

She reflected on this. Doubtless thinking of her position.

'Would I be much help?' she said. 'They'd ask me about your drunken days. And I'd have to tell them.'

'I never killed anyone when I was with you.'

'I nearly killed you,' she said.

They were quiet a while. He, and no doubt she, thinking of their last difficult years together. His alcoholic stupidity, his homelessness...

'They are going to be moving you, I hear,' she said.

'Some time tomorrow. After I come back from the magistrates court, I leave the police station and get taken to a jail. Some huge dump somewhere.'

'I hope not far. Mia wants to see you, me too. We'll work it out, wherever it is. In the meantime, me, Mia and Nova are meeting tonight to work out what we can do for you.' She looked at her watch, and rose. 'I must go.'

He said, 'American author, died 1888, Louisa May something or other. Daily Mirror crossword.'

'Alcott,' she said. 'Wrote *Little Women*.'

Chapter 14

Nova entered the office. The smell of perfume almost got her sneezing. She squeezed her nose and sucked in her breath; this was no time for a fit of sneezes. DI Hawley was at her desk, working on her laptop. The room was just large enough for her desk and chair, a cupboard behind her and a visitor's chair. As an added luxury, she had an outside frosted window.

Hawley looked up and glanced at her watch. 'I haven't got long, DC Taylor, but this won't take more than a few minutes.'

Nova wasn't being invited to sit down, so she steeled herself for the worst. She knew this was due, before being called here, and had thought about what she must say. Half truths and lies.

'You went to visit Jack Bell.'

She had been right. This was it. Though it didn't take much detective work.

'I did,' she said, clutching her fingers tightly behind her back. 'I needed information on a drug deal.'

'Tosh!' Hawley threw up her hands. 'You are in a relationship with him, DC Taylor.' She glared at Nova. 'So you went to see him to give him information on the murder he has been charged with.'

'I gave him no information, ma'am.' Almost true. 'I told him that as a police officer I couldn't see him again.'

Lie number one.

'Your visit was a direct interference with my case.'

Nova had known this. But felt she couldn't simply disappear from Jack's life. She'd had to see him.

'Sorry, ma'am.'

60

'Sorry is somewhat thin gruel, DC Taylor.' She slapped her desk. 'Let's get down to the nitty gritty. How long have you been going out with Jack Bell?'

Where was this going? She'd best take care.

'About ten months,' said Nova, 'though on and off, as I have been very busy.'

'When was the last time you saw him?'

'Four days ago. Jack and I went for a walk round the lakes in Wanstead Park. I meant to see him last night, a date at the Stratford Picturehouse, but I had to get some paperwork to the CPS urgently. I lost track of time and phoned to cancel. Jack was outside the cinema waiting for me.'

'How do you know he was outside the cinema?'

'He said so.'

'Don't be naive, DC Taylor. He could have been anywhere.'

She was about to protest. She'd been due to meet Jack at 7.30 pm. Whether he was at the Picturehouse or not, it hardly mattered, as the events on Wanstead Flats had happened after 11 pm. She stifled her riposte, and waited for her superior.

'You will have to be questioned formally, DC Taylor. And I suggest you have no further dealings with Jack Bell. It would only make matters worse as I have put in a complaint against you of gross misconduct.'

That hit her so hard, she could barely breathe.

'Did you say gross misconduct?' she managed to say.

'You have interfered with an active murder investigation by visiting him.'

'Hardly interfered,' she said weakly.

'You will be interviewed here by an advisor to the complaints panel, DC Taylor. If they consider there is a case to answer, you will go before the panel where your case will be judged.'

'I could be dismissed,' she said, struggling to hold back tears.

'You should have thought of that before lying your way in to collude with your lover. Who just happens to be on a murder charge.'

'I told him nothing he could use.'

Hawley shrugged. 'Let the panel decide that. Enough chit chat, DC Taylor.' She looked at her watch. 'Now get out of my sight.'

Nova stared at her accuser, there was no mercy in those eyes. She would be another of Hawley's results. About to justify herself, she quelled it as pointless.

'Thank you for your time, ma'am.'

She turned and left the room. In the corridor, she had to support herself against the wall, as the implications sank in. A complaint of gross misconduct. Once the machinery began to roll, it could not be stopped. This was devastating. She knew of others who had been before the panel, and most of them had been dismissed.

Nova had worked hard to become a detective. Had she thrown it all away in one act of stupidity? She'd never get another job with gross misconduct against her name.

All for a visit to Jack.

Chapter 15

DC Alagia was driving, Hawley in the passenger seat by him. They were on the way, against the flow of rush hour traffic, to Stratford. He had the window open as he found her perfume cloying, even though it was raining quite hard.

Darts of rain splashed on the road and washed into the flowing gutters. The windscreen wipers flashed back and forth, like line dancers. Alagia didn't speak but concentrated on driving. His boss' face was grim. She wouldn't welcome any interruption.

He thought of Jack Bell, his repeated declarations of innocence. That meant little. He'd done it himself as a kid, swore blind he hadn't broken a window, until it was proved that he did. The declaration was neither here nor there. It was the motive that bothered him. Bell was in a relationship with Mrs Litt. Which he denied. Had to, in order to maintain his plea of innocence.

OK, so he's her lover. Why kill her husband?

A fight between husband and lover, maybe. But why would the builder have a gun? Not a usual item in his toolbox. Could have been Mr Litt's, then it becomes self defence. Or another tack, Mrs Litt had made Bell a promise if he killed her husband. A promise she was going back on.

She certainly wouldn't admit it, and nor could Jack if he stuck to his claim of innocence. The various possibilities should have been meat and drink between him and his boss. But discussion wasn't her way. She said what was what. And if he disagreed, it was ridiculed. He'd learnt the hard way to shut up.

He'd thought at first she'd be a good boss. She got results; he'd be part of a winning team. But she worked non-stop and expected the same of him. Stress was her middle name. The last month, he'd been sleeping badly, been bad tempered with his wife and kids. All unfair. It was not their fault he had a pushy boss.

It was his hope that her promotion would come through shortly, and he'd be partnered with someone more amenable. She'd told him that DC Taylor was up for a complaint, and dismissal was a likely outcome. Which would mean Taylor's boss, Inspector Fayyad Kamani, would be seeking a sidekick. Kamani was a nice guy. He smiled sometimes and even allowed disagreement, if you could back it up. A good cricketer too, which was why the Super liked him.

He must speak to Kamani. Not yet. Wait for his boss's promotion and Taylor's dismissal. Let it come quick, his boss was driving him crackers.

He turned into Water Lane, aptly named in this weather, and took the first left, to the entrance of Sarah Bonnell school. He stopped the car, got out into the pelting rain, and spoke into the entrance intercom.

'Detective Inspector Kate Hawley has arrived.'

Two girls dashed outside the front doors with raised umbrellas. They carried another one each. They gave one to him and the other to Hawley as she stepped regally out of the vehicle.

'Thank you, girls.'

'This way, sir, madam,' said one of the girls. A black girl, 15 or so. 'You are just in time.'

'I told you, Ben,' said Hawley to her sidekick.

He didn't reply, as what was the point? He always came early to things, she was a 'just in time' person, and frequently late.

Once inside, the girls took the umbrellas, and slipped away, their role over. The school principal was waiting for them. She was a middle-aged Asian woman in a red and orange sari, her almost-black hair below her shoulders.

'So glad you could make it, Inspector.'

'Detective Inspector. Please get my rank correct when you introduce me.'

'My apologies, Detective Inspector. So sorry about the weather. Please come this way.'

She led them through double doors into a large hall, full of ranks of seated pupils and parents. Alagia stayed at the back of the hall. He was just the chauffeur. He was offered a seat but chose to stand.

Hawley and the Principal went down the mid aisle to the stage where teachers and dignitaries were seated. It reminded him of his school days, when he'd played trumpet in the school orchestra on occasions like this. Once in a while, he took the instrument out and played a few tunes. The Met had a jazz band he would have liked to join, but detective work made such regular outings impossible.

Hawley and the Principal were on stage, behind them the half circle of seated dignitaries.

At the mic, the Principal addressed the audience. 'It is my pleasure to introduce a former pupil, Detective Inspector Kate Hawley, who is now at Forest Gate Police station. Can we give her a big hand of applause!'

Applause swept the audience.

The Principal stepped back, leaving Hawley at the mic.

'Thank you, thank you,' she said as the applause began to ease. She held up a hand for silence. 'Thank you, girls, parents and teachers.' She turned behind her, 'Governors and Mayor.'

She looked out into the ranks, their eyes on her, waiting for her. This had been a minor ambition when she sat on those seats as a schoolgirl, to be guest speaker on Founders Day. A little vanity, but not a vice in her eyes, but a spur to greater ambitions.

'I was at this school twenty years ago,' she said. 'We lived at Henniker Point, Maryland. I could get to school if I really shifted in eight minutes. And frequently, I waited until 8.32 am, and hared along.'

Alagia smiled. So there was the origin of her last minute rush. But walking was one thing, a car journey lacked the certainty.

'I left Sarah Bonnell and went to Newham Sixth Form College,' continued Hawley. 'And then onto Newcastle University where I studied history. I loved history, still do, it puts the world in perspective, but unless you want to work in a museum or teach, it is not a gateway to employment. So I applied to the police force.

'Since that time, I have worked my way up from probationer with days at police college, to police constable, and then specialised in criminal investigation. After more study, I became a detective constable, and after several years I was promoted to detective sergeant, and now I am at the rank of detective inspector in the serious crime squad. I am currently completing course work to become a Chief Inspector.

'I make no apology for my ambition. I am aiming high as I suggest all you girls should be. There are less and less barriers to women's aspirations these day. Marriage was never part of my career plan. I do not want children.'

She looked along the ranks of the audience to let her controversial sentiment sink in.

'There is a myth of happy families, too often repeated.' She flicked a dismissive hand. 'Hoo-ey! In my job I come across unhappy families. Battered wives, murdered wives, abused children, physically and sexually, murdered husbands, misery, unhappiness and squalor. Nor am I letting the well-to do off the hook. I have arrested enough of them, for murder and serious violence, to not be fazed by a cut-glass accent.

'You might say I am biased, seeing so much of the seamy side of human life, and I admit it, I most surely am biased. As I reiterate, I am a career police woman, I do not want children. There are 8 billion people on the planet. The world does not need another child, from me or from you. You may want a child, that is your choice, but you are not doing the world a favour, rather you and your family are consuming valuable resources with each extra child.'

She swung her arm across the audience.

'You might be somewhat shocked by me, girls. But I make no apology. Your life is your own. It does not belong to your family. Remember this, if you remember nothing else I have said today. Make your life worth living. You are not simply here to breed children like a swollen queen bee. Be ambitious. Make a name for yourself. Do something in the world. Don't die a nobody.'

Chapter 16

Mia and Alison were completing the cooking when Nova arrived. The meal was the house stand-by for quick eats. In the freezer was a stack of Margarita pizzas, which they'd embellish. Tonight they were adding red peppers, olives and onions. Mia completed hers with oregano and pepper as she was a vegetarian, heading on vegan, while Alison added thin slices of pepperoni sausage to the other.

With the pizzas in the oven, they sat at the kitchen table and drank coffee. Alison said wine was not a good start for a serious meeting. Nova might have argued, but then again, the way she was feeling, she could have consumed the bottle and gone for a second.

Mia hadn't been to school that day and was dressed in jeans and a loose red top. Her mother had arrived after one of her endless meetings, so was still dressed in role, in her check suit, simply taking the jacket off. Nova, in her navy blue dress suit, removed her jacket too. Two career women, but on different rungs of the ladder. Alison nearing the top, while Nova was close to toppling off.

'I'm in trouble,' said Nova. She did so long for the wine she could see on the counter.

'What for?' asked Mia.

'For visiting your father,' she said. 'I lied to get in, a crazy lie. But I had to see him. And now I am on a complaint for gross misconduct.'

'That is serious,' said Alison, who knew of these things from her school's complaints procedure. 'Are you likely to be suspended?'

'Very likely. And soon.'

'That is so unfair,' declared Mia. 'Dad is innocent until proved guilty and allowed visitors.'

'True, and not true,' said Nova. 'Your mum can visit, but I am a serving police officer, a detective, and have no right to interfere with other cases.'

'So why did you risk it?' said Alison.

Nova screwed her face. 'I thought it would simply be ignored. Or I might get a reprimand. I didn't allow for Detective Inspector Hawley. She is an ultra disciplinarian, and doesn't like my boss.'

'Oh, Fayyad,' declared Mia. 'He's dishy.'

'Why doesn't she like him?' said Alison.

'He's a favourite of the Superintendent. She's a cricket umpire and he's a star batsman for the Met.' She laughed. 'See how it works? And Hawley hates him for it.'

Alison was taking the pizzas out of the oven.

'Office politics,' sighed Alison. 'Isn't it sad how petty things can get.'

'So what could happen to you?' said Mia, as she gathered plates and cutlery from the cupboards.

'I'll be suspended in the next few days. That's a near certainty. Then I hang about at home, prepare my case with a Police Federation representative, and in a few months I go before the panel. Up London somewhere. I shall have my rep with me. It's like a trial, with prosecution and defence. Then the panel decides what to do with me.' She took a deep breath before continuing. 'I could be let off. The least likely outcome, as those cases don't usually get to the panel. Or I could be given a final warning.'

'What does that mean?' said Mia.

'It means if I'm caught taking so much as taking a canteen teaspoon, it's curtains. The warning lasts two years or so, and would be on my record for evermore. Or, I could be demoted. For me that means losing detective status and being back in uniform. I'd hate that but it's better than dismissal which is the ultimate punishment, and is handed out in the majority of cases before the panel. They take no prisoners.'

'Hawley could have turned a blind eye,' said Alison.

'Would you have?' said Nova.

Alison placed the two pizzas on large dishes, and put them on the table, steaming with mozzarella and oregano. Mia sliced them. A job she delighted in, as it suited her geometric bent.

'Depends on the case,' said Alison. 'Please help yourself, Nova. There's only tap water...'

Mia had filled a jug from the tap and was putting out glasses.

'It's a thousand times cheaper than bottled water,' she said. 'Most people can't tell the difference, no matter what they say. And all those bottles thrown away or recycled, which is such a poor option.'

'We get this every day,' said Alison.

'You got rid of the water cooler at your school,' pointed out Mia.

'OK, OK, I concede,' she raised her palms in submission. 'If we are going to be green, we have to start in the staff room.'

'You were telling me what you'd do with someone like me.'

They had all taken slices of pizza and were eating.

'I'd look at your past record to start with. Then I'd talk to you. Is it a one-off or are you likely to do it again? And then I'd decide. I wouldn't want to start the complaints procedure if I could possibly help it. That's such a chore, expensive too.' She flapped her hands at the thought. 'A panel, union reps. These things can go on and on. And no-one wins in the end.' She took a drink of water. 'If you had a good record, I'd give you a final warning, and you could go back to the classroom. If you had a history of transgression, I'd give you the option of resigning.'

'Thanks for nothing.'

'You did ask. Besides which, the cases are not really comparable. Teaching and policing. Well,' she reflected, 'some things in common. I have been to schools where you feel more like a cop than a teacher.' She took the last slice of pepperoni pizza. 'In your case, clean record, I would give you a warning.'

Nova smiled. She knew what Alison was doing. Not giving offence where she didn't have to.

'What are we going to do about Dad?' said Mia. 'He's way past a final warning.'

Chapter 17

They had settled in the sitting room with coffee, and followed up with chocolate ice cream and banana. As they sipped and scooped, they got down to the real business of the evening.

'Mrs Litt is the crux,' said Nova. 'She is insistent that Jack was having an affair with her.'

'He denies it,' said Alison. 'And I believe him.'

'So do I,' said Nova.

'Suppose he really was,' said Mia. The two women looked at her aghast. 'I am just supposing. That's allowed, isn't it?'

Alison blew out her cheeks in exasperation. 'My daughter.'

'Just supposing, OK,' said Nova. 'Sex and murder often go together. Toss money in and you increase the likelihood of dirty work.'

'Moses supposes,' began Alison, 'that Mrs Litt wants Jack to kill her husband, so offers him inducements. Sex, money...' She stopped. 'I don't want to play Cluedo. Jack wasn't having an affair with her. Full stop. Wouldn't you know if he was, Nova?'

Nova smiled wryly. 'I have had lovers who fooled me for months. And I have done it myself. Not recently, I may add.'

'She's a liar,' said Mia adamantly. When Nova looked at her wide-eyed, she added, 'Not you. Mrs Litt. I bet she has a lover. The two of them killed her husband, and are framing Dad.'

'Stacks of possibilities,' said Nova. 'Story books of them. But they are Just-So stories without evidence.'

'We need to talk to her,' said Alison. 'But I doubt she'd be willing to talk to us. What's in it for her? I mean, I can't just ring her doorbell, and, when she opens up, say, Mrs Litt, I'd like to have a word with you about your husband's murder.'

'We could kidnap her,' said Mia.

'And beat her up,' said Nova wryly, 'until she confessed.'

'There's a truth drug,' began Mia.

'No, there isn't,' cut in Nova.

They were silent, eating their ice cream, feeling it a little incongruous with Jack locked up, and the evidence against him piling up.

'I have a way of getting to her,' said Nova, contemplating as she spooned her ice cream. 'It's risky, but I think I can swing it. I know her FLO. Family liaison officer. It's her job to keep Mrs Litt in touch with developments in the case. Her FLO owes me a favour. I'll see if I can persuade her to let me go and see Mrs Litt instead of her. Just the once. '

'That's a risk,' said Alison. 'You're already in deep trouble. On a complaint for gross misconduct.'

'Well, if I am going to be dismissed...' she laughed, 'I might as well go for broke.'

'It's no laughing matter,' said Alison severely. 'If you go and see her, and you are found out, they'll sack you on the spot.'

'So I'd best not get found out.'

'I can't allow it,' said Alison.

'She's not one of your students, Mum,' protested Mia.

'Think about it, Alison. I'm on a complaint. With the very real risk of dismissal. And why? Because I'm a detective, and I went to see a man charged with murder. In a case I should be having no part in. But suppose we can prove he didn't do it?'

'How?' said Alison.

'Don't know. Yet. But if we can, then the complaint against me is weakened. Looks malicious, even.' She faced the two of them, excitement in her eyes. 'Don't you see? Think of my defence if we prove Jack innocent. My rep would say I went to see Jack because I believed him to be innocent and Hawley, the investigating officer, was barking up the wrong tree. And hey presto! When we have proved him blameless, the complaint evaporates.'

'I think you have leapt a few squares,' said Alison.

'What do you suggest?'

Nova and Mia turned to her.

Alison shrugged. 'I feel quite useless. I don't know what to do.' She threw out her hands helplessly. 'I'm a school principal. I can't condone breaking rules.'

'Never, ever?' pressed Nova.

'I can't stop you,' she said weakly. 'But...'

'Oh, don't be so woolly, Mum.' She turned to Nova and waved her spoon. 'Go and see Mrs Litt. Put her on the spot.'

Nova smiled at her earnestness. 'You have the casting vote, Alison.'

'I can't give a say-so which could get you sacked,' she said. 'I am sorry. Stupidly sorry, but I really can't.'

'Two in favour,' said Mia. 'One on the fence.'

Chapter 18

Jack had been given bedding: two sheets, a pillow and a duvet. He'd taken his time making the bench into his bed, not being on piece-rate. At some unnamed hour, the light went out, leaving a faint blue glow in the ceiling. Enough to make out shapes, to get to the toilet if need be.

He got into bed. It wasn't uncomfortable but it was stuffy in the cell. He liked a window open in the night. Not an option in this windowless space.

There was a commotion in the corridor. Someone was being locked up for something, and obviously unhappy about it. There was swearing, bodies hitting floor and walls, yelling from police officers. It sounded like a rampaging army out there. Though it could be just a drunk and lots of cops piling in.

He'd had experience.

A cell door banged, followed by yelling and kicking of the door. The occupant next door wasn't giving up. A man, aggressive, sounded drunk and stupid. Jack could hear the cops going away, laughing and calling back. The occupant could bang and swear till the cows came home; they were paying him no heed. Like a crying baby, left to cry himself out.

A bedlam of swear words and crashing against the door followed. Building to a crescendo, dying down, then building again in fury and rant, and on and on.

It was giving Jack a headache.

After maybe twenty minutes of his neighbour's fury, Jack rose from his bedding. In the near-darkness, he could make out his suitcase. He opened it, felt around, and found the pack of earplugs which he had dismissed earlier. He put one in each ear.

Better than nothing.

The sound was less piercing. Still annoying. The man couldn't be doing his shoulder any good, crashing against that door. Metal door in a metal frame; it didn't require a builder to realise the flesh and bone of the human body was a useless battering ram. Drunks are idiots. His swear words were rather limited. Cops were this, that and the other. Or the other, this and that.

Jack could almost agree. Some cops at least. But the man was going on and on, and the point had been made.

No point yelling, shut up! It would just stir the man up. Let him rant and get no reaction, eventually even his fuzzy brain would realise there was no point in his frenzy.

Earplugs dulled the noise, but there was still too much racket to sleep. He would need those noise reduction earphones. Alison had a pair she used on flights. She might loan them, then again, expensive headphones wouldn't last five minutes in clink. Someone would steal them, and no insurance would pay up.

Had he been this bad in his drunken days? Likely. Drunks don't give a damn. Too insensible to care about the consequences, which was the point of getting drunk. And staying drunk, and being picked up by ambulances and cops, hitting them, swearing your head off at them, life being too demanding to stay sober.

The yelling stopped. My god in heaven. Could it last?

After a few minutes, Jack was pretty sure that it was at an end. Likely the man was fast asleep. Jack took out the earplugs and put them under the pillow. In the blessed quiet, Jack reflected on his day, more like a month of days, beginning at six in the morning with his arrest. In a flick of handcuffs, he'd gone from solid citizen to a man on a murder charge. His clothes taken away as evidence, given baggy substitutes. He had had two interviews, thrown that senseless punch, had visits from Nova and Alison.

And he'd got clothing and shoes, reading matter, a notebook. He could shave in the morning, clean his teeth, make himself presentable for the magistrate's court. He would like a watch; they had taken his when he arrived. Though, would he spend all day looking at it? Wondering why the hands dragged, when lunch would come, when tea, when supper.

It was helplessness that sapped the soul.

Nova and Alison had met tonight to discuss what to do. Mia there too, practically grown up. She'd had to witness his arrest. He wanted to talk to her. Alison had said she would bring her on a visit.

Bring her when, where? Tomorrow, he'd go to magistrate's court. First stop. A formality, he'd been told, as they would send the case to crown court, in heaven knows how many months time. After magistrate's court, some time tomorrow, he'd be taken to a jail. It could be in London, it could be two hundred miles away.

He had a lawyer. Alison had got him one. Good old Alison; they'd had their battles, but she was standing by him. All was forgiven. And Nova would know how the case against him was progressing. So there were possibilities, stark as they may be.

Alison and Nova were his eyes and ears on the outside. They could investigate whereas he, in this cell, or any other cell in a place as yet unknown, could do damn all but think what he couldn't do.

Jack hardly slept. It was stuffy, there was too much to think about. Too much he could do little about. In the early hours, he got up, and did his repetitive ramble. Door to wall, wall to door, repeat ad infinitum. He wouldn't count the laps, as that was distracting. Then couldn't stop, and losing track. And so what? His aim was to tire himself out, so he could sleep.

He had a little shut-eye, a couple of hours he reckoned, waking when the light came back on. Jack was still stretching when a prison officer brought him breakfast. It was 7 am, he was told. And at 9, he was going to magistrates court.

Rice Krispies in a one-person pack, milk, sugar, beans on toast and a cup of tea. He began with the beans on toast, they had a remnant of warmth. Then the Rice Krispies and tea.

Breakfast done with, he washed, cleaned his teeth and shaved. Then sorted some clothes out, not the greatest of choices, and wondered how clothing got washed in prison. Did you do it yourself, or did it all go in a monster wash? If the latter, how did you ever get your own gear back?

All would be revealed.

Washed and dressed, and nothing happening, he waited for the man. He was in his box, while decisions were made about him. He was keeping a lot of people in work, though not willingly. Cops investigating, cops guarding, cops doing paperwork, IT people making spreadsheets, forensics in their coveralls crawling all over his flat, lab workers investigating fibres and pollen grains. Soon he'd be providing work for the courts of the land.

And journalists, don't forget media. The ever-hungry maw, like a squawking nestling, must be forever fed with titbits, gossip, scandal, murder and mayhem.

At last, he mattered in the world.

Jack tried reading yesterday's newspaper, and gave up. A thought came to him, how he might use the paper to get a message out. Spies did that with an agreed book. He'd seen it in a film; the book had been Pride and Prejudice. The spy had sent rows of numbers, each row referring to a page, a paragraph, a sentence and a word.

His thoughts rambled on like a fly on a window. Nova or Alison could try to talk to Mrs Litt. But she would lie, of course, if they could even get to her. She had her tale, it had satisfied Hawley, but there might be cracks in it.

Time ached in this place.

Eventually, two police officers in uniform came for him. Neither of whom he had seen before. Another shift of officers presumably. Jack was handcuffed and led out of the cell.

Chapter 19

He was led along the corridors and out of the police station. In the car park, he was put in a mini-van. There were six officers already in it. Jack was put in a seat, and the two who had escorted him from the cell, took their places in the van.

Eight officers with him. He couldn't believe the number.

'Why so many of you?'

'In case you try anything,' said the officer next to him.

'I'm a peace-loving man,' he said.

'You hit a DI yesterday,' said the officer.

Jack was going to say he hadn't hit anyone, but realised it wasn't these cops he needed to convince of anything. They were simply his escort. No, not escort, they were there to protect the public from a dangerous murderer. They were his guards.

The talk around him was about the canteen food. The chips were soggy, the eggs overdone, sausages burnt, the tea was always stewed. He was a little surprised by the criticism. The meals had been better than he thought they'd be, then again his standards were pretty low.

Two officers tried to defend the canteen and got shouted down. It was like a school bus. The loud and the subdued. He was the most subdued, as he didn't feel they'd welcome his comments on the canteen. Nor was it high in his regard.

He had other fish to fry this morning.

The van drove off. The traffic was busy. Jack knew the route well enough, along the Romford Road. Past what had been the Princess Alice, a lousy pub in its day, no wonder it went under, past the mosque in what had been a cinema, the Muslim girls' school that had been a church of some ilk, he couldn't recall which. The leisure centre with wet-haired youngsters coming out with rolled towels under their arms.

The everyday world.

It was cloudy, a few blue patches, not enough for the telescope which remained in their keeping, presumably thoroughly dusted for fingerprints and DNA. To a passer-by on the pavement, he looked normal enough gazing out the van window. Admittedly, the only one person out of uniform. Maybe they thought he was a detective, if they thought at all. They couldn't see the handcuffs.

In less than ten minutes, they had arrived at Stratford magistrate's court. In the car park, he was let out of the van, and taken into the court with his entourage of officers. The cuffs were briefly removed at the metal detector, and put on again at the other side.

They were in a wide corridor with a number of courts on one side, indicated by double doors and a uniformed attendant at each. Across the corridor on the other side were high windows. It was light and airy, with a babble of conversation from groups huddled around each court door.

Jack was taken to court 4. There, he was approached by a smart, plumpish, middle-aged black woman. She was in a striking green trouser suit, her dark brown hair in a topknot, bound with a matching green ribbon. She had a folder under her arm.

'Jack Bell,' she said.

'That's me.'

'Jo Innes,' she said. 'I won't try to shake your hand with those cuffs. Take it that I have.'

He took it that way. She looked efficient. She'd been here waiting. Good sign, and she wasn't intimidated by the group of cops he was with.

She turned to the police officers. 'Can you please give us space? I wish to speak to my client in privacy.'

The officers backed off. She sat on a bench at the side of the court door, and beckoned him to join her.

'I have never seen so many cops with a client before,' she said. 'You must be dangerous.'

'They exaggerate,' he said.

'They frequently do. It says here,' she indicated a paper she'd removed from her folder, 'that you struck an inspector.'

'I attempted to.'

'Please don't do it again if you want me to represent you. They make too much of such things and it biases the jury against you.'

'So I have been told too many times.'

'Never too many,' she said, with a hint of a smile. 'You are charged with murder, Jack. Are you innocent or guilty?' She held up a warning finger. 'Not that you will have to plead today. All cases start at magistrate's court, but yours will be passed on to crown court which deals with serious cases. So, how will you plead once we get there?'

'Not guilty.'

'Fine. That helps me prepare your case. A plea of guilty and we'd be sorting out mitigation. With a plea of not guilty, I shall be looking for every speck of evidence why you couldn't have done it.'

'Mrs Litt is lying.'

Jo Innes raised a hand. 'I am not familiar with your case, Jack. I was only taken on yesterday afternoon. But don't worry, I shall be up to speed very quickly. All that gets decided here today is whether the case goes to crown court. Frankly, it will. This is all a waste of time really, for me, all these officers and for you.'

'I have plenty of time to waste,' he said. 'It's an outing.'

She smiled, then switched to lawyer mode. 'My fee is being paid by Alison Bell. What's her relationship to you?'

'Ex-wife.'

'I'm glad you still get on.' She smiled. He enjoyed her smiles. She was treating him as a human being, an innocent one. Or was that just her pose? Her work mode.

'I note, she's a school principal. Would make a good character witness.'

She might not, thought Jack, but didn't say so.

The double doors opened and the attendant beckoned them inside. Jack went in with Jo, four cops following, the others remaining in the corridor in case he intended to break out.

Jo led him to a bench with a table in front. Behind them were tiers of benches, presumably for the curious, for relatives and friends of the accused and the victim. Jo put her folder on the table and took out a large notebook.

Others were coming in, some filling the benches behind him. DI Hawley entered, glancing at Jack, behind her came DC Alagia. Then four people who sat at the central table.

'Press,' said Jo. 'Your murder isn't big enough to have much of the media here.'

'It isn't my murder,' he said. 'I'm innocent. Remember.'

'Don't get heated,' she said. 'A slip of the tongue.'

Three magistrates were seated in high backed chairs on a dais behind a wooden wall, hiding their lower bodies. Two women were on either side of a man, each had fixed mic on the table surface before them. The man was in a suit, late middle age, almost bald. One of the women wore a hijab, the other had red hair, obviously dyed. They chatted quietly, eyeing him. He was important.

A woman at floor level handed the centre magistrate some papers. Behind the magisterial threesome was a large portrait of the King when young.

There were high windows in the court room, like a church and lots of dark wood panelling. A babble of conversation as if everyone was wondering where the bride was.

'Mrs Litt isn't here,' he said quietly.

'The widow, I assume.' Jack nodded. 'It's neither here nor there. This isn't a trial. This is simply to say where you will be tried.'

'And everyone knows that already.'

82

'We do. But I suppose it's useful in that we get to see faces. The characters in the drama. We'll have to wait for the widow. That table there, that's the prosecutor. Though they have probably just sent a junior to this first hearing.'

The centre magistrate banged a gavel. So he was the front man, Mr Big. He was quite stout, a family butcher perhaps, thought Jack.

'Call the accused.'

Two policemen came and escorted Jack to the witness box. The handcuffs were obvious to everyone watching. He was their focus. A dangerous man.

Jack climbed the few steps into the box.

'Please take the oath, sir,' said the magistrate into his mic.

An official handed Jack a card. He read it into his mic.

'I do solemnly, sincerely and truly declare and affirm that the evidence I shall give shall be the truth, the whole truth and nothing but the truth.'

He was asked his name, his date of birth, address and profession.

He gave the information and noted, one of the press was sketching. She'd have to be quick as he couldn't believe he'd be here long. She kept looking at him, then down to her pad, her lips screwed in concentration. Apart from the professionals, there were maybe fifteen members of the public on the benches. He wondered who they were. Did they know the victim, or were they just curious members of the public and he was the big case of the day?

Two cops were by the box and two at the door.

No chance of escape then.

'You may step down, Mr Bell.'

'I am innocent,' he said to the magistrates and assembly. 'This is all a big mistake.'

'That's as may be, Mr Bell,' said the main man. 'But this is not the time or place to make your case.'

The magistrate in the hijab smiled, whether at his error or in sympathy, he had no idea. She was probably a mother, so maybe the latter. Not that it mattered, but smiles were smiles. He couldn't get too many in his situation.

Jack was escorted from the box, back to his place by Jo Innes, who was writing notes.

'Everything I told them they knew already,' he said.

Jo shrugged. 'Court procedures are very repetitive.'

DI Hawley was in the box. She took the oath and was asked to identify herself.

'I am Detective Inspector Kate Hawley of Forest Gate Police Station.'

She was smart in a navy blue dress suit. A hint of make-up. Not too much, she was a cop after all.

'We have heard from the accused. What is the charge, DI Hawley?'

'Jack Bell is charged with the premeditated murder of Thomas Litt.'

'Can you give an outline of your evidence?'

'The accused Jack Bell was having an affair with Yvonne Litt, the wife of the victim. Blood has been found in Bell's van. The victim was found by Bell on Wanstead Flats. He had gone there with his telescope.'

'A bird watcher,' said the centre magistrate.

'No, sir. It was late at night. The telescope was an astronomical one. For stargazing.'

'Will the instrument be produced in evidence?'

'Yes, sir. Bell says he was looking at the stars when he heard the victim cry for help, which is why he went to his aid, he says. But the victim had been dead for many hours. Obviously a lie. Bell's van was nearby and, as I have said, found to have blood inside.'

It was as if the magistrate and the cop were talking about someone else. A conversation between old friends that Jack was listening into, as if on the seat behind them on a bus. What he thought was immaterial. The truth belonged to them. It would be rude to interrupt.

He was stuck in a process that once on the move was impossible to halt. Reputations were involved, and would be protected at any cost. He was but another log floating downstream to the sawmill.

Jack couldn't see the members of the public. They had a clear view of his back, but the media bench watched him, as if he might give himself away by some gesture. Two had laptops they were typing into, an older man had a notebook. The sketcher, her face screwed in concentration, sketched on.

'Clearly a case for crown court,' said the chief magistrate. His two colleagues nodded. 'Is the accused represented?'

Jo stood up. 'Yes, sir. I am Josephine Innes, solicitor. I'd like to apply for bail.'

The chief magistrate turned to Hawley, who had remained in the witness box. 'What is the police view?'

'We oppose bail on the grounds that the accused is a dangerous criminal and, if released on bail, may well threaten witnesses.'

'Bail denied,' said the chief magistrate. 'Jack Bell, you are remanded in custody. The case of the Crown versus Jack Bell is sent to crown court. Thank you, everyone in attendance. If we can clear the court of those involved in this case, we can proceed with the morning's other business.'

Chapter 20

Jack was taken back to the van with his attendant entourage. In the van, on the short trip back to Forest Gate police station, the talk was of football, last night's game between Manchester City and West Ham. At some other time, he might have taken an interest, being a West Ham supporter, going a few times a year to see them at the London Stadium, but any interest was blown far by the winds of fate.

Jack had been told how it would go at magistrate's court, and it had gone that way exactly. But it was the inevitability, the realization, that he was shackled to a process that had its own speed, and cared not a jot for him. He would be jailed, regardless of his protests of innocence, of a miscarriage of justice. The magistrates had commanded that he be remanded in custody until the case had its time in crown court. That could easily be a year or more.

He could barely breathe in the football babble around him. For the cops this was a pleasant interlude, an outing, it just needed someone to pass round the doughnuts. But for him, a life-crushing hour. It had been decided, he would be jailed until a jury decided he would be freed or locked up for life. Even if found not guilty in a year's time, he would lose his flat. And that was the shiny side of the coin.

There were too many cases of wrongful imprisonment. Who knew actually how many? There were those eventually freed on appeal, and those who never were, their lives ruined. Once someone was charged, police and prosecutors worked night and day to demonstrate their guilt, no matter the truth. It was their truth only that mattered.

Such a nightmare.

At the police station, he was taken to the interview suite. There, Jo was waiting for him. She had driven ahead. Still in handcuffs, he sat on the sofa, she at the other end. A policeman was on guard at the door.

'Nothing unexpected at court,' she said.

'It's a factory,' he said. 'With lots of well-paid people whose job is to find me guilty.'

Jo shrugged. 'It's the way of things. We can't change the justice system. They have a case they aim to prove. While we will do our best to disprove it.'

'Whatever happens, I'm in the clink for a year.'

'Unless they decide they have made a mistake.'

'How often does that occur?'

'Sometimes. Not often. The court and cops don't like backtracking. It's human nature. We don't readily admit we have made a mistake.'

'I am so depressed,' he said, his head sank into his hands. 'I knew what was going to occur this morning. I'd been told by the custody solicitors. But you don't feel it, till it happens. All those cops coming with me to court, talking about how dreadful the food is in their canteen, the magistrate telling me I am remanded in custody. And me driven back here with the same cops talking football, and I'm all the time in handcuffs, utterly stitched up.'

Jo put a hand on his shoulder. 'We have some unstitching to do, Jack.'

He looked up and nodded. Someone on his side in this cage of malice.

'Let's hear your side,' she said. 'Tell me exactly what happened on Wanstead Flats.'

Jack could hardly bear to retell the tale, it had been condemned as a pack of lies. He groaned, rubbed his eyes, stretched his arms, took a deep breath and began the saga, beginning with him at his telescope around 11 pm. Then hearing the cry for help, and searching for the source. Finding the body, realising it was his client, calling the police and the ambulance, and all at once he was a suspect, with van and telescope confiscated. Going home, annoyed at his treatment, only to be arrested and charged in the early morning.

Jo was taking notes in her large pad, asking the odd question.

'The blood in the van,' she said. 'Has it been tested?'

'It's the same blood group as Tom Litt. But hasn't been DNA tested yet.' He threw out his elbows, restrained by the cuffs, indicating inevitability. 'It will be his, of course. Some random guy's blood in my van makes less sense than a frame up.'

He told her about Mrs Litt. Her fabrication of their affair, claiming they went to bed every day, while Tom was out at work, and Jack was meant to be bricklaying.

'Why is she lying?' said Jo, banging the pen on her pad.

Jack half laughed. 'Don't I want an answer to that one. She's at the heart of the frame up.'

'A strange situation she's in,' mused Jo. 'Sleeping with the accused, according to her, and then grieving the victim. No wonder she wasn't in court today. The lady is running with the hare and chasing with the hounds. It's puzzling.' She put her notebook down. 'A point in our favour. Her two-faced muddle. I would so like to hear her tale.'

'What I was like in bed,' said Jack, half grinning, but little humour in it.

Jo proceeded to pack up. 'We'll get to see her statement. And anything else the prosecution has. All in due time.' She rose. 'I'll be with you for any further questioning by the police. In the meantime, I'll get what I can out of the Crown Prosecution Office.'

A woman police officer in uniform entered.

'Excuse me interrupting,' she said, 'But Jack Bell has to get his things together. He is going to Parkhurst prison in an hour.'

'Did you say Parkhurst?' said Jo, aghast.

Jack had heard of Parkhurst, but had no idea where it was.

'I did, ma'am. Parkhurst, on the Isle of Wight.'

Jack now joined in the alarm.

'That's miles away,' he exclaimed. 'How am I to get any visitors?'

The officer shrugged. 'I'm just the messenger, sir.'

Jo turned to him. 'Do not pack your things, Jack. You are not going to Parkhurst. It would take me three hours at least to get there, the same back. That's a whole day to see you for an hour. How can I prepare your case with that mammoth journey every time I need to speak to you?'

'It's part of the stitch up,' he said. 'Get me so far away, I can't defend myself properly.'

'Stay here,' said Jo. She turned to the police officer. 'Who told you Jack was going to Parkhurst?'

'The custody officer, ma'am.'

'Let's start there. Take me to him.'

Chapter 21

Jo strode into the custody officer's domain. He was at his desk in his small office, a middle-aged man, grey-haired and portly. Desk jobs evidently extended the waistband.

He looked up from his computer at the interruption from this belligerent black woman.

'It's polite to knock,' he said.

'It's polite to keep prisoners remanded in custody in a local jail,' she retorted. 'Did you authorise Jack Bell going to Parkhurst?'

'Nope. I took the order and passed it down the chain. It's my job to get the prisoner ready for transport.'

'So who authorised it?'

'That would be the Chief Superintendent.'

'I need to see him or her.'

'With respect, she doesn't need to see you.'

'Are you obstructing me?'

'No, ma'am. Just telling you that you can't go barging around a police station as if it was your own home.'

Jo reflected. Aggression wouldn't work. Not with this man. She needed to back off and get him on her side. Or Jack would be packed in a van and taken far away. She'd then have to fight to have him brought back. Weeks of phone calls, letters, and emails. She knew how stubborn the system could be.

'I need your help,' she said. 'It's not fair for my client to be taken out of the London area. I have to prepare his defence.'

'You have a tough job on.'

'I most surely do. Made all the tougher if my client is on the Isle of Wight.'

'I get that.'

Quite what he got was difficult to fathom. He most likely thought Jack guilty as he had been charged by one of their own. So any problems she or Jack had, just pile 'em on.

'Would you please contact the Chief Superintendent?' In her gentlest, most reasonable voice. 'I'd be most grateful. And tell her I must speak to her about Jack Bell being taken to Parkhurst.'

The duty sergeant reflected for a few seconds. He could stonewall her or pass her on. Which would give him less hassle? He knew her sort. Pushy solicitors. She wouldn't stop until Hell froze over. Frankly, he couldn't care less where Jack went, so long as he left the station and cleared a cell.

An Asian man stepped into the office. He was slim, wearing a smart dark grey suit and a red tie.

'Excuse me interrupting, Sam,' he said, 'but is it right they are sending Jack Bell to Parkhurst?'

'It is, sir.'

Jo turned to face the newcomer.

'I'm Jo Innes, Jack Bell's solicitor. I am objecting to him being taken so far away.'

'I'm DI Kamani. I know Jack. It's not my case, and I mustn't interfere. But I don't understand why a prisoner remanded in custody is being sent to Parkhurst. Do you know why, Sam?'

'No, sir.'

'The Chief Superintendent made the order,' said Jo. 'I'd like to talk to her. Get her to reverse the order.'

Kamani thought for a second.

'I'll take you to her office. Then it's up to you.'

'I'd be grateful.'

He picked up the phone on the custody sergeant's desk.

'DI Kamani, ma'am. I have the solicitor for Jack Bell with me...'

A few minutes later, Jo was in Chief Superintendent Nikki Martin's office. Rank obviously enhanced the space and furniture. The room was the largest she had seen in the station, with an expanse of desk suitable for her status. There were several chairs and a small sofa, a window with orange curtains overlooking the station car park, a low bookshelf with trophies and medals in frames. One trophy had a woman cricketer in silver on a stand, padded up, her bat out at shoulder height as if to smash a ball for six.

Nikki Martin was behind the desk, in a dazzling white shirt. She was stocky, middle-aged, with short blonde hair. Her hair was natural in colour, the grey hardly showing, she wore the lightest of make-up.

She looked at her watch. 'I must be away in five minutes. This concerns Jack Bell?'

'Yes, ma'am.' Jo was aware she was with a higher-ranked officer. She could be brusque down the line but it wouldn't pay off here. 'He has been remanded in custody. I am his solicitor. How can I defend him if he goes to Parkhurst?'

'I know Jack,' mused Nikki Martin. 'He has helped us a few times. DI Fayyad Kamani is an old friend of his. I was surprised to hear he's been charged with murder.' She flapped a hand in dismissal of her doubts. 'But the evidence is mounting up against him.'

'Who authorised he be sent to Parkhurst?' said Jo, adding as an afterthought, 'ma'am.'

'It would have been me. I sign lots of papers. Too many. Yesterday afternoon, it must have been. Yes, I'm sure of it. Magistrate's court is a formality in murder cases, so it was set he'd be taken to prison straight afterwards.'

'But why so far away? Three to four hours' drive from London, just as long by train. A ferry crossing too.'

'Prisons are busy, overcrowded. We send prisoners where there is space.'

Jo took a deep breath. She'd have to be pushy, no matter the rank.

'You realise, ma'am, I will have to call you as a witness in court to justify that decision. Making his defence more difficult.' She looked about her, caught sight of the trophies. 'It's just not cricket, ma'am.'

A classic strike. She knew the ball park, if not the fact that Nikki Martin was a cricket umpire for the Met.

Nikki Martin smiled. 'Do you play?'

'I was a runner at University. 400 metres. Though my brother is a fast bowler for Wanstead.' He wasn't. She just knew there was a club there. 'You aim to win,' Jo went on, 'but you must play fair.'

The Chief Superintendent nodded, and picked up her phone.

'Joan,' she said on the phone, 'who set up Jack Bell to go to Parkhurst?'

Jo watched as the Chief Superintendent spoke to her secretary. Cricket had swung her over. Though it might assist Jack, if the police were to be seen obstructing his case. On another level it would weaken his case, if she were unable to see him because of the time involved in getting to him.

Nikki Martin put down the phone. 'DI Hawley set it up.'

'The senior investigating officer!' Jo threw up her hands. 'I simply don't believe this. The senior investigating officer is obstructing Jack Bell's defence. That's intolerable. I shall have to call you both as witnesses. You will have to justify why you sent him so far away, and so weakening his defence. And I certainly would use it if we have to go to appeal.'

'I dare say you would,' said Martin, getting the measure of the woman before her. 'Jack Bell has a good lawyer. He'll certainly need one, from what I hear.'

'There are lots of London prisons, ma'am. I've been to four of them for various cases. A little phoning around and space could be found, surely.'

'No need to rehearse your witness box questioning. I agree with you, I should not have signed the paper. But I am reversing it. Jack Bell is staying here for the time being. I shall have a word with DI Hawley, and we'll sort out a London jail.'

Chapter 22

Jack was put back in his cell. He wasn't going anywhere, he was told. At least not today. Jo left him a Guardian newspaper. Plenty to read, the weather forecast, puzzles and two crosswords. One cryptic which made no sense to him, and a simple one which he found wasn't so simple.

Turning a page, his face peered out at him amidst an article. Murder on Wanstead Flats was the headline. Where had they got that terrible photo from? Not many facts, just that the body of Tom Litt, a Forest Gate property developer, had been found on the Flats, and local builder, Jack Bell, who was said to be having an affair with Mrs Litt, had been charged with his murder.

Not much in the Guardian, but he knew the tabloids would hype it to heaven. They'd love the sex angle. What they didn't know, they'd make up. Get snippets from neighbours and anyone who'd ever passed him in the street.

If he ever got out, what was the chance of getting any work ever?

Jack was brought tea and biscuits by a copper he recognised. The shifts go round and come back again. In fact, the officer had been in the van that had taken Jack to and from the magistrate's court.

'Your solicitor caused a stir,' said the officer.

'That's because I am innocent.'

'I'm not working on the case, sir. So I can't say what you are. But I do know a van arrived, a few minutes ago, destination Isle of Wight. Full of bods from other stations, and a ticket for Jack Bell. They got sent on their way with one empty seat.'

'I didn't fancy the seaside,' said Jack. 'I like smelly old London air.'

'I've done a bit of cycling round the island.'

'I don't suppose that's an option for inmates of Parkhurst.'

'Talking of options, would you like to tick what you'd like for lunch?'

He gave Jack a menu.

'Let's see what we have today.' He began ticking items. 'It's not so bad, this grub. You guys were having a moan on the way to court.'

'It gets a bit samey. I doubt you'll be bothered as I reckon you'll be off tomorrow.'

He took the menu and left.

Busy morning. The way not to dwell on your troubles. Keep moving. He could almost get used to Forest Gate nick. The food was OK, he'd only been beaten up once and that was his own fault. The handcuffs were a nuisance when he had a visitor. No phone, oh, he could do with that. And no natural light.

The officer returned.

'You have a visitor, Jack.'

He was handcuffed once more and taken to the custody suite. To his surprise, there was Mia.

Once they were seated, he said quietly, so as not to be overheard by the officer seated at the door, 'How did you get in?'

She shrugged. 'I told them at the front desk I was 18. They wanted proof, but Fayyad came by. Piece of luck, that. And he said, let her in.'

'Good old Fayyad.'

'How are you, Dad?'

'All the better for seeing you.'

'What happened in court? I was thinking of going, but I got waylaid by things.'

'Shouldn't you be in school?'

He'd noted she was not in school uniform, obvious she was taking another day off, wearing jeans with a floppy green top which had the motto: *There's no Planet B.*

'I thought school can go hang, I'll come and see you. Get you up to date. First things first: Nova can't come any more. She's been charged with gross misconduct for coming to see you.'

'It was just a visit,' he protested. 'Nothing more. She never told me anything I could use.'

'She thinks she'll get suspended. Could lose her job.'

'That's so unfair. We just talked.' He threw his hands in the air. 'This place, I don't believe it. They hit you with one thing after another. Out of the blue.'

Another relationship done for. Not that it stood much of a chance, with him inside till his case came up. She'd been one of the best. When he got to see her.

Mia looked around at the police officer by the door.

Quietly, she said, 'Nova is going to see Mrs Litt.'

'That'll get her in deeper trouble.'

'That's what Mum said. But Nova reckons if we can get evidence that you didn't do it, they'll drop charges against her.'

Jack pondered on this, but there were too many ifs and ands to get far.

'I've been thinking,' said Mia. 'We've all been concentrating on Mrs Litt and her lies.'

'We have to find out why she's lying,' said Jack. 'And bust it in half. The cops have lapped it up.'

'So have the papers. In the Sun, you are a 'Love Killer'. Another reason I didn't go to school.'

DI Hawley had warned him, when she urged him to confess, that his whole family would be hit by the publicity.

'Mum is getting lots of phone calls,' went on Mia. 'The scum media assume your ex would be happy to dish the dirt on you. Mum just puts the phone down. But that's not what I want to talk about.'

'What then, if it's not Killer Love Rat Dad?'

'That's not funny,' she exclaimed. 'I'm getting all this stuff on social media. Some of it, so disgusting. They think, if you've been arrested, you must be guilty, and must have abused me and beat up Mum.'

'There's some advantages to being in jail without a phone.'

He thought of the media at his door if he was free. Stuck indoors because of the circus outside.

'Mum says I can take a week off school while the heat dies off.' A tear rolled down her face. 'Some people are dreadful. I've had about a hundred emails this morning...' She gave a half laugh. 'They make it sound like I was the killer. I put you up to it. And I must be horrible to be in the same family.'

'Sorry, love.'

What could he do? Not a damn thing. People got hysterical, egged on by the tabloids.

'I'm not blaming you, just stupid people without a brain cell between them. And oh yes,' she changed the subject, to get away from the tabloids and fellow travellers. 'There's cops on Wanstead Flats,' she said. 'I went over to look. They've taped off an area. I saw a TV camera, and this woman with a microphone. I kept well away. Wouldn't do to get on TV.'

'I am getting tried before I ever get to court.'

'You're guilty, they all say. The case is slam dunk proved, a one way ticket to a life sentence.'

'The cops are feeding the media, I am sure of it. Setting it up, so every member of the jury knows the verdict before the case starts.'

'That's always the way,' exclaimed Mia. 'That's what they do. The Feds. Fit you up and bias everyone against you.'

Jack held up his hands. 'Can you ease back? I feel like I'm being kicked all over.'

'Sorry, Dad. But you would find out what's in the papers and on TV, anyway.' She threw her hands up. 'Let's forget social media and the fuzz. I'm here to tell you what I've been thinking.'

He waited. His 17 year old daughter was an impetuous eco-warrior. On his side, thank heavens. She might have wild conspiracy theories but could be quite sharp on occasions. He hoped this was one of them.

'We've all been talking about her, Mrs Litt, the liar. But what about him? The victim. Tom Litt. You didn't kill him. So who did? She was at the theatre, it says in the Sun. Her alibi. But she could have hired a hit man... Then again, she might not have done.'

'Go on.' He had been down this road and didn't want to put words in her mouth.

'Let's suppose she didn't hire anyone. In fact, she had nothing to do with the killing. That means someone else killed Tom Litt and then put the frighteners on her to fix you as the fall guy.'

'You should write crime books.'

She screwed up her face at the put down.

'This is the point,' she said, 'the heart of it, Dad. Listen to me.' She shook a fist at him, as if he wasn't. 'Why would someone want to kill Tom Litt? Who had he so vexed?'

Chapter 23

It was a sunny, late morning; Nova came through the gate of the house on Hampton Road. Double frontage, Victorian, in the conservation area of Forest Gate. Two wide windows, either side of the path, two storeys and mock pillars by the door. These properties were going for well over a million. Mrs Litt wasn't working so Tom Litt must have been doing well.

What did she do at home all day? Apart from taking builders as lovers.

There were two cars in the drive. Presumably one hers, one his. There were large ceramic containers with tulips, and some flowering shrubs, azaleas were they? Her aunt had some. There was a monstrous plant in front of one of the windows with limbs like a sea monster out to engulf the house and contents.

Jack always said, you could learn a lot about the occupants by just looking at their house. If the repair was kept up, the roof, the state of the curtains, the cars. She guessed Mrs Litt took care of the garden. All the time she had. No kids. There'd be a big garden at the back, where Jack had been working. Long thick, drawn curtains, posher than blinds. The house would be spotless, she was sure.

Hardly Jack's type.

There was a large clay container, about a metre high, to one side of the door, containing some shrubby plant not yet in flower. Nova tilted it. Underneath was a pair of keys.

Careless, asking for a break in. She suspected Mrs Litt was the nervous sort, afraid of losing her keys. Maybe Tom Litt was a bully and she wouldn't want to be sitting on the doorstep when he got home, telling him she'd lost her keys.

Enough Sherlock Holmes deduction. Remember the keys for another day. She rang the bell. It echoed through the hallway. She waited maybe twenty seconds, was about to ring again when she heard footsteps in the hall. Nova took a deep breath. She had to win Mrs Litt over and get what she could from her.

The door opened. A tall woman stood there. She was slim, with dark brown, straight hair just below her shoulders. She was wearing jeans, and an apron over a blue t-shirt. Her hands were encased in red rubber gloves almost up to her elbows. In one hand, she held a large sponge.

'Hello,' said Nova with her friendliest smile. 'I'm Nova Taylor from Forest Gate police station.' She showed her ID card which Mrs Litt looked at closely. 'Patsy, your FLO, is ill I'm afraid. So I am deputising, just for today, to keep you up to date with the investigation.'

Patsy wasn't ill. Just reluctantly paying back a favour.

'You are not in uniform,' said Mrs Litt.

'I'm a detective constable,' she said. 'Plain clothes. I don't normally do family liaison work these days, but I did in the past. A big investigation has just finished, and I was asked if I could fill in for Patsy.'

Would she ever get in? All she was doing was telling her prepared fibs.

'Have there been developments?'

'There have. Can I come in?'

Mrs Litt hesitated, her face twitchy, thinking perhaps of an excuse to close the door on her. The woman was definitely nervous, and why wouldn't she be? A murder case resting on her pack of lies.

'Come in,' she said reluctantly. 'Let's go in the garden.'

Nova followed her through the wide hallway, tidy as she'd guessed. They passed the stairs, at the top was a vacuum cleaner and large washing up bowl with various plastic bottles in it, which she surmised were cleaning liquids. The lady was giving the upstairs a good scrub up.

They continued down the hallway, through the house, and stepped out of the back door into the garden.

The garden was the width of the house, and maybe one and a half times as long. Much of the garden was lawn, with beds on either side against the fence, filled with shrubs and flowers. Along the back fence was a shrubbery, with a shed at one end and a greenhouse at the other.

'I see you are giving upstairs a good clean,' said Nova.

'I am scrubbing the bedroom from top to bottom,' she said. 'I want to clean out every atom of that dreadful man.'

Jack, of course, being the man in question. He was saying that he had never ever been in her bedroom, and forensic testing would show no sign of him there. No DNA and no fingerprints. But according to Mrs Litt that would be so, because she was cleaning away every atom of his presence.

Purely her word against his.

'Take a seat,' said Mrs Litt. 'I'll make us some tea.'

She went into the house, leaving Nova on the patio. She realised she was so far, even less help to Jack, as she was a witness to Mrs Litt's clean up. And now she was gone to make tea, probably needing to escape, to calm herself, and keep her story straight for this new FLO. Not a natural liar, so why was she putting herself through it? She'd be hammered in the witness box. Though she could break down, play the grieving widow. All the more damning for Jack. But if he had actually been sleeping with her...

A traitorous thought. Mrs Litt alone in the house, her husband at work. In her garden was a builder whose girlfriend was non-stop busy. Pair them up on computer dating. Nova shook herself, she was doing the prosecutions work for them. But she had doubts, not that she dared admit them to Jack, but the situation could have been just too tempting.

And so he murdered her husband.

At that, the fantasy of an affair, of Jack bedding her every day, evaporated. One thing she was sure, Jack wasn't a killer. So working backwards from that certainty, no affair.

Not so fast.

There could still have been an affair if he was not the killer. Such a tale held. The randy builder scenario simply helped the real killer with the fit up. That would mean Mrs Litt wasn't a complete liar when it came to Jack. Suppose their affair was part of the set up. She seduced him to frame him. Meaning she was hand in glove with the killer. The lady was too slight to be moving bodies.

Supposition on supposition, pull out a card and it all topples.

Nova sat at the ironwork table on the patio. In front of her was the wall Jack was building. About three feet high, with a gap of about 15 inches and a parallel second wall. She supposed the space between the two walls would be filled with soil, and tumbling flowers planted. About two thirds finished. There was a string line along the brickwork, and a toolbox, most likely Jack's. There was a pile of fancy bricks at one end of the patio, which presumably would go on top.

Jack had been here for three weeks. They must have become lovers pretty sharpish, according to Mrs Litt's tale. In that short period, he had become so enamoured that he had killed the husband so he could have her to himself, or so she fabricated. And DI Hawley took on board, hook, line and sinker.

Mrs Litt returned with a tray containing a tea pot, mugs, a milk jug, a plate of chocolate biscuits and her iPhone. She placed the tray on the table and sat down. She had removed the plastic gloves and apron, no doubt to return to her scrubbing once Nova had left.

'A lovely garden, you have here.'

A safe area of discourse.

'Thank you,' said Mrs Litt. 'I was hoping we could get the building work done, so I could enter Forest Gate Garden Trail this year.' Nova looked puzzled. 'It's when various gardens are opened up to the public. They make a map of the trail. It's lots of fun, they tell me. You meet so many people. But that's out the window. With Tom dead. And Jack

Bell in prison for his murder. The last thing I want is hundreds of over-curious visitors traipsing through.'

'I quite understand. This is all a trial for you.'

'There's a write up in The Times, we, I mean I,' she sniffed tearfully at her change of pronouns, 'get it delivered. Difficult to come to terms with just me. By myself in this big house. All his stuff everywhere. In the wardrobe, his books on the shelves, the bathroom with his shaving gear and lotions, everywhere I look.' Tears filled her eyes which she struggled to control. 'Please, excuse me.'

'Of course,' said Nova. 'It's just a few days. I am so sorry we have to intrude.'

'I'll have to register the death, and when the body is released, I'll have to arrange a funeral...'

'Have you no other relative who could stay awhile?'

'I'm an only child. My parents are in Spain, though my mother will be coming over. I'm not sure whether that is a good thing or not.'

She poured two teas. 'Help yourself to milk, Nova. Thank you so much for coming.'

Nova wondered about that. Then again, she was company, and not pressing her. Not yet. Just being a sympathetic listener.

'The story in The Times about the murder,' Mrs Litt shuddered as she spoke, 'I turned the page and there was a photo of Jack Bell. It quite shook me.'

'It's in all the papers,' said Nova. 'An area of Wanstead Flats is now a crime scene, TV were there for the Breakfast Show this morning. They showed us going house to house in the hope of finding anyone who might have seen or heard something relevant.'

Nova had scanned the newspapers and looked at Holmes, the police computer system, before setting off, to get herself up to date on the investigation and the media's intrusion. She poured milk into her mug and sipped her tea. It didn't feel right to take a chocolate biscuit in front of a weeping woman. Mrs Litt had dark rings round her eyes.

She obviously wasn't sleeping well. Guilt or grief? Or maybe fear.

She must go gently. Be a friend. The role of the FLO. Somewhat deceitful, listen and be sympathetic, and report back anything untoward.

'The blood in his van,' said Nova, 'DNA testing has shown it to be your husband's without doubt.'

That was a lie. DNA results hadn't yet come back from the lab. But she felt she had to have some new development to justify her visit. It could get her in trouble if the blood wasn't Tom Litt's, just a handy stranger's. And she could be disciplined for it, even if it was for her prematurity.

Dismissed twice. She was making sure they'd get her one way or another.

'How he fooled me,' said Mrs Litt. 'I was too easily swept up by his passion. I admit it, utter stupidity. He flattered me. I was like a weak-kneed teenager. I know that's no excuse, but I am certain my husband had someone on the side. There was perfume on his shirt, he was always working late, very late. So me, stuck here, alone all day, was it any surprise I was tempted?'

That's a speech, she had off pat, thought Nova. How many times had she said it already? And would repeat endlessly.

'You were a victim,' said Nova, keeping up her sympathy mode, 'here alone, he's a good-looking man. And utterly ruthless.'

'Men can be such liars.'

Nova almost laughed at this insult to the male sex. Here were two women drinking tea and lying their heads off. She knew well enough, from her detective work, neither sex had a monopoly on lies.

She discreetly pressed record on her phone.

'Something is puzzling us,' said Nova. 'A little thing you might be able to help with, Mrs Litt.'

'Yvonne. You don't need to be so formal. We are having tea and chatting. It's not a council meeting.'

'Yvonne,' went on Nova. 'The cat's head on Jack's thigh. This.'

She held up her phone and showed an image of thigh and tattoo of a cat's head covering much of it, while covering the red recording light with her thumb.

'He won't say anything about it,' said Nova. 'He just clams up. Did he tell you its meaning?'

Nova watched her closely. There was no cat's head on Jack's thigh. As his lover, she would swear to that in the highest court in the land. Or at the Pearly Gates. She had pulled the image from the internet. A cat's head on a hairy thigh.

She hoped she was recording, but did not dare take her thumb off the recording light to check. She had thrown in her ace, and now awaited Mrs Litt's response.

Mrs Litt looked away.

'He wouldn't tell me,' she said. 'I asked him a couple of times, and then gave up. Something he feels guilty about.' She shrugged. 'Another dirty deed, I don't know.'

'We think it might be connected with another murder,' said Nova. 'We are investigating.'

She was lying for England.

'I have no idea about that tattoo. He wouldn't say. How I wish I had never met him!'

Bingo! Nova had got her on the cat. A cheap ruse, but it told her Mrs Litt was lying about her affair with Jack. Any lover would know, he had no tattoos. The recording was hard evidence, though got by deception. Would it be accepted in court? The prosecution would fight to have to have it excluded. But at least she knew where she was. The woman was a liar.

More importantly, for her at least, Jack was telling the truth.

'What will happen to Jack Bell?' said Mrs Litt.

'The evidence is piling up against him,' she said. 'The blood in his van, your evidence of an affair, his shaky tale of what went on on the Flats, I can't see how a jury would not find him guilty.'

'What would be his sentence?'

'Premeditated murder. 30 years, I'd say. Though the cat, if that is connected to another murder we are investigating... He could get a whole life tariff. And will never leave prison.'

Mrs Litt was shaking uncontrollably. 'Excuse me. I must go to the toilet.'

She rushed into the house.

Once alone, Nova turned off record on her phone and sent the file to Alison. Then turned off her phone. She had noted that she and Mrs Litt had identical iPhones. Easy to mix them up.

She put her phone by Mrs Litt's place and pocketed the other.

A mistake anyone might make.

Chapter 24

Jack had had lunch and was playing with his pen, taking it to bits, working out how the retraction worked, and putting it back together. Clever and cheap, 12 for a quid at the pound shop. Now what? He could do with a jigsaw puzzle or a pack of cards. Something to take care of time. Meals and visits were his only distraction.

When his meal had gone down, he'd do some exercises. Wasn't he entitled to time outside? Though where? The few cells at the station were just for temporary stays. They had no exercise yard. There was just the car park and he doubted they would risk him out there.

He went on his weary walk, thinking inevitably about the case. How he was tied in as the murderer. By Mrs Litt's tale of an affair, by the planted blood in his van. He often left it open when he was working, anyone could have got to it, watched him a while and, when he was occupied, taken their opportunity. The cry on the Flats was obviously to draw him over, to find the corpse of his employer, shot dead several hours before.

And that was all he knew. What he'd done, what they said he'd done. But what actually happened was conjecture on conjecture. And he was in the clink, reliant on others to investigate, while detectives and forensics piled up the evidence against him.

Mia reckoned it could all be about Tom Litt, the victim. He'd been up to some dirty work and got his comeuppance.

As good a story as any.

Jack dropped onto the bench, utterly weary of Forest Gate nick. Just this cell, the day only enlivened by visitors. Worse than being in hospital. He was on remand, and so, at least, he had the privilege of more visitors. No one yet had been turned away, as far as he knew. Even Mia had got in. Lied about her age, but she did that often enough, as he had done at 17 to get into clubs and to drink. He'd even had fake ID which he'd bought for a tenner.

On his notepad, Jack worked out a series of scenarios, and was just beginning to list their pros and cons, when he was told he had a visitor. He was handcuffed, the usual palaver, and taken to the interview suite. Alison was there with a large bag.

'They are still handcuffing you,' she said with a frown, on seeing his shackles.

'Once they have decided something,' he said, 'it takes an earthquake to reverse it. I shall be handcuffed until doomsday. Anyway, thanks for coming.'

'I've taken a long lunch hour,' she said. Which he'd known at once from her greenish tweed dress-suit and sensible shoes. School principal wear.

'Any news from anyone anywhere?' he said, eager for anything to give a chink of hope.

'Could well be,' she said. 'But let me give you this lot.' She drew items out of the large bag she had with her. 'A jigsaw puzzle of Mia's, a pack of cards. I hope I am not offending you with these games.'

'Why would you be?'

'Normalising jail.'

'I am very grateful. Anything to break the boredom,' he said, looking at the jigsaw puzzle picture on the box, 500 pieces of The Haywain by John Constable. A lot of cloud and a wagon in a river. That would keep him busy. 'I'm going nuts here. They're not even bothering to interview me any more. I've nothing to tell them beyond what I've already said, and they didn't listen anyway. Now I'm just taking up space. Tomorrow, I'll be off, to some London jail.'

'I've brought you some fruit, satsumas and bananas. Healthy,' she said with a sly grin, knowing his aversion to that adjective. 'And a book, I thought you'd need something to get your teeth into. I know you don't read fiction, so I hope this works.'

She gave him a thick tome, Are We Alone in the Universe?

Jack laughed. 'I most surely am.'

'It's astronomy,' she insisted. 'Your passion.'

'Got me in here in the first place,' he said. 'There I was, out on the Flats with my scope, alone in the Universe, and then...' He stopped, aware he was being ungrateful. 'Thank you for the book, Alison.' He glanced at the blurb, a mixture of astronomy, biology and physics. 'Looks fine, might well be up my street. Thank you, wonder woman.'

'Shut up. We may not be married, but I am certain you are not a killer.'

'I am grateful. You don't know how much. But you said there was some news. Good even?'

Alison shrugged. 'I don't know the full ins and outs, but Nova went to see Mrs Litt, told her a pack of lies to get in, which I hope doesn't get her in more trouble. Anyway, she made a recording which she sent to me, I haven't had time to listen to it, being at work, meetings, admin, oh, and prison visits, buying astronomy books... She says it proves you weren't having an affair with Mrs Litt.'

Jack was taken aback. 'My God. You sure?'

'That's what she said. We are having a meeting at my place at five, after school. I can listen then to the recording, and one of us can come in tomorrow morning and fill you in.'

'I won't sleep tonight.' He shrugged, 'Not that I am sleeping well in that stuffy cell. Soon as I go back in after a visit, I'm overpowered by the smell of sweat and urine. Then I get used to it. Like a pig in a sty.'

'I must leave you, Jack,' she said, glancing at her watch. 'A hundred things to do before the coven meets.'

Chapter 25

Nova was in a plush office in Stratford, with a view of the Olympic Park from its 8th floor window. She was seated at one side of a large desk. The man across from her, in a higher swivel seat, was Asian, in his mid 30s, wearing a grey, well-fitting suit, with a light blue shirt and a navy blue tie. He was slim, his almost-black hair receding.

There was a cycle machine, alongside shelving units, with a large photo of him on top, utterly exhausted in running gear, coming through the finishing arch of the London Marathon. On the desk was a metal name piece: Tahir Ahmed, in case you'd forgotten who you had come to see.

'I wondered when the cops were going to arrive,' he said, in an East London accent rubbed smooth by education.

From which she gathered, DI Hawley had not bothered to come here, having more than enough on Jack Bell. Good, this was virgin territory. She shouldn't be here, interfering in another's case, but with luck Hawley wouldn't find out.

Nova had taken the afternoon off, on condition she came into the station in the evening to complete her paperwork on the case she'd been working on. It had been pushed aside in her need to help Jack. There was guilt in that. She had doubted his faithfulness. Her knowledge of men, her knowledge of herself. There was love for her hapless builder. Trouble stalked him. And she was joining him, courting trouble for his sake. She might well be drummed out of the force for gross misconduct.

'How long were you and Tom Litt partners, Mr Ahmed?'

'Call me Tahir.' He stretched his legs in ownership, his brown brogues on his desk. 'Eleven years or so,' he said. 'We met at Cass Business School as it was called. Now known as Bayes, whoever he was, Cass having been toppled due to his involvement in the slave trade in the 18th century. A philanthropist at home, a slaver abroad. The dirty underbelly of the British Empire.'

He laughed, a little superior, as his ancestors weren't slavers but under the heel of Empire.

'You have done well,' she said, looking about the office and noting the view.

'Pretty well,' he said smugly. 'Tom had a great eye for land. And could talk the hind legs off a donkey. He was so tenacious in going for a deal.' He snapped his fingers. 'I knew at once he was the guy to team up with when I first spoke to him at college. We were determined not to get stuck in merchant banking, making Coutts and Co even richer, but to get out into the jungle and make it ourselves. Boy, we played fast and loose to get on that first rung. I wouldn't dare tell you some of the things we got up to, but you've got to have money to make money.'

He chortled, obviously dwelling on his buccaneering exploits.

'So what happens to the business now?' she said. 'Now Tom Litt has gone.'

He shrugged. 'That leaves me in sole ownership. Not as good as it sounds, as there were two of us, with our own portfolios, out and about making deals. I shall have to take someone on. Maybe two. Not as a partner, oh no, but I need a couple of sharp boys or girls, I am not sexist, to keep the wheels on the bus going round and round.'

She almost added, all day long, but instead said, 'How does Mrs Litt fit in?'

'She inherits her husband's shares, which is 25% of the business, which makes her quite a catch, but she has no control. Not that she needs any. The business is doing well.'

He stroked his nose to indicate his shrewdness.

'The name, Litt and Ahmed. Will you change it?'

He shrugged. 'I am considering Lbut letting it sit a while. It's early days.'

'You've benefited considerably from your partner's death. One might suspect you had a hand in it.'

Ahmed sat up, taking his feet off the desk, obviously affronted.

'Am I a suspect?'

'Everyone is at this stage,' she said. The old cliché. But Ahmed had a ruthless streak. He might laugh and joke, but pity anyone owing him money. 'Can you tell me where you were on Tuesday?'

'Tuesday, Tuesday,' he considered. He suddenly brightened, 'I was down in Worthing for much of the day. Set off about 7am. A lovely piece of land, covered in weeds, and crying out for development. I tell you this, trade secret, two thirds of the time, you hang on to it for a few years, and then sell on without laying a brick. Rising market,' he threw his hands out, 'why build?'

'I'd like you to send me details of your time in Worthing,' she said. 'What did you do in the evening?'

'It was Arsenal v Manchester City, a cup match at the Emerites.' He scowled. 'We lost. That last-minute penalty was ridiculous. I swear the ref was in their pay. Waste of two hours. The match finished about 9.30, I got home around 10.30. You can ask my wife.'

'I will. Where's home?'

'We have a flat in the Barbican.'

Far enough from Wanstead Flats to rule him out, if true. Though if he was responsible for his partner's death, Ahmed was not likely to do it himself. He'd hire a hitman, and make sure he had a watertight alibi. Which, it appeared, he had.

'Did you and Tom socialise?'

'Not much these days. I'm married with a young daughter.' He laughed at what he was about to add. 'And Tom kept himself busy.'

'He was having an affair?'

Ahmed blew out his cheeks. 'And how! Not that it bothered me. He could shag Nelson's Column and the four lions so long as he brought the money in. His secretary, two years plus it's been going on. Time they had a new carpet in the office.' He chuckled.

'I'd like to speak with her.'

Chapter 26

This office was plush too. On the thick, olive-green carpet, there were two desks: Tom's Litt's, the obvious large one, and the secretary's, smaller with a computer. Under the wide window, there was a long sofa.

Sarah Raban was buxom, wearing flat shoes, her heels under her desk, with a short skirt, and a buttoned green jacket top. She was immaculately made-up with thick purple lipstick as if habit was too strong for her to dress down.

Her expensive perfume filled the room.

From a shelf with a cafetiere, she'd made Nova a coffee. They sat on the sofa, their mugs on the low glass table in front of them.

'You've been fired, I hear,' said Nova.

'Been made redundant,' Sarah corrected her with a slight smile. Her dental work was perfect, dazzlingly white. 'Mr Ahmed has promised me an excellent reference.'

Nova noted the touch of resentment.

'You were having an affair with Tom Litt?'

She shrugged. 'No secrets round here. He was my boss and my lover. This sofa has been well used, I can tell you. It pulls out into a bed.'

Nova couldn't help a smirk.

'You don't have to look at me like that. I am a very good PA.'

And good at other things, thought Nova.

'How did it work out with Tom Litt?' she said. 'As his PA and lover. Tricky sorting out work and er... pleasure.'

Sarah smiled wryly. 'I don't recommend it. It's an uncomfortable relationship. He has all the power. And let's not mince words, he was a bully. And I was trapped. Not at first. I was recruited as his PA, the affair developed. Willingly, I wasn't coerced into it. There was lots of late working, well into the evening, and you know how these things happen with a little wine.'

'So it started fine. Then what?'

She laughed. 'We worked late, went out for dinner, came back here. I was his wife, more than his wife was, for all he saw of her. He upped my salary; I am on 70 thou a year.'

Prostitution, thought Nova, more or less.

'I needed that cash. I had to dress for him, and be up for it any time he wanted, and then take a letter. There's a shower in that bathroom suite.' She swung her arm round the office. 'All laid on for work and post-work. That wardrobe,' she pointed it out, 'my dresses and accoutrements.' She shrugged. 'I won't miss this place. It got to be drudgery, his bullying. The hours! But the pay was good, that's what I'll miss, I'd bought a flat and needed the money coming in to keep up the mortgage.' She threw her hands wide. 'If I'd upped and left any time, I'd have got a lousy reference and where would I earn money like this again?'

'I see the drawbacks,' said Nova.

'The other girls here, they stop speaking whenever I come in. I know they've been talking about me. They have various names for me. None of them flattering. So no bad thing, I'm out the door. It's got him off my back. No pun intended.' She took a sip of coffee. 'I want to be just a secretary, a PA, fancy word for the same thing. Leave at five without the girls gossiping about me.'

Nova was not unsympathetic. No means a dream situation. Very well paid, but with a bully for a boss and lover. And despised by the rest of the staff.

'Did Tom Litt have any enemies?'

She smiled wryly. 'Of course he did. He'd screw the last penny out of his grandmother. Machiavelli would have taken notes.'

Nova had vaguely heard of Machiavelli, the last word in ruthlessness.

'Tom ducked and dived, lied and lied. Anything not on paper, he'd welsh on. A promise was a means to an end, to be broken if it suited him. Oh yes, he was well hated. By me, amongst others. Do you want chapter and verse?'

'I certainly do,' said Nova. 'Can you email me a list of those he screwed over, and we can talk them through on the phone?'

'Happy to do so. I don't owe this firm a thing.'

Chapter 27

Alison and Mia were at home in the kitchen. Mia was making a salad, Alison chopping carrots to go with French beans.

'I'm in two minds about you staying home any longer,' she said.

'It'd be terrible at school.' Mia took on a silly voice: 'What's it like having a murderer for a father, Mia?'

'And what would you say?'

'No point saying anything. There's too many of them.' She stopped slicing tomatoes. 'We have to get Dad off. And not just for his sake.'

Alison put the beans and carrots on the stove to boil. She glanced at the wall clock. 'Where's Nova? I left early especially for our get-together.'

'She went to see Mrs Litt, didn't she?'

Alison clicked her fingers. 'She did, she did. And sent me a recording. Let's listen.' She busied herself attaching her phone to her laptop, found the file and clicked.

The two speakers were easy to distinguish. Nova had quite a deep voice, while Mrs Litt's was higher and more refined.

Nova: Something is puzzling us. A little thing you might be able to help with, Mrs Litt.

Mrs Litt: Yvonne. You don't need to be so formal. We are having tea and chatting. It's not a council meeting.

Nova: Yvonne. The cat's head on Jack's thigh. This. [Pause] He won't say what it means. He just clams up. Did he tell you its meaning?

[A long pause]

Mrs Litt: He wouldn't tell me. I asked him a couple of times, and then gave up. Something he feels guilty about. [Pause] Another dirty deed, I don't know.

Nova: We think it might be connected with another murder. We are investigating.

Mrs Litt: I have no idea about that tattoo. He wouldn't say. How I wish I had never met him!

The recording went on a little longer, but off the subject of the tattoo, then halted.

'Play it again,' said Mia.

The doorbell rang. Alison left and came back with Nova as the recording played for the second time.

'Sorry I'm late,' said Nova.

'Shh!' hissed Mia.

The recording played through. Alison clicked it off.

'I assume Jack has not got a cat tattoo on his thigh since our divorce,' she said.

'He hasn't. I found a picture on the internet of a cat's head on a hairy thigh.'

'Show us,' said Mia.

'I can't,' said Nova. 'I swapped phones.'

Mia and Alison looked at her in puzzlement.

'Explain,' she said, turning on the microwave to bake the potatoes.

'We have the same phone, me and Mrs Litt. So I swapped them over while she was in the loo. Mine was turned off, so she'll just think there's some techno fault when she can't get in. Hers was turned on, I had a quick look but had other business to get on with. I saw some emails that needed explaining, but didn't have time to explore further. And when I got back to it, it was off and I couldn't get in.' She half laughed. 'Can't be helped, I've been ultra busy today. I've left the phone with an IT guy at the station, told him to keep mum as this is totally unofficial.'

'Another reason to fire you,' said Alison.

'That makes at least three,' said Nova. She enumerated on her fingers. 'One – visiting Jack when I'm not on his case.

Two – seeing Mrs Litt, saying I'm an FLO. Three – stealing her phone.' She sank into a chair. 'And there might be four, five and six. I've been looking at Holmes, the police computer, to keep up to date. The gun used to kill Tom Litt, they think it is an Italian model. A Penna 7mm, very unusual round here. So would be worth asking the right people, who happen to be the wrong people, where you might get one.'

The table was set, and in a few minutes, they were eating: baked potato with butter, grated cheese or sour cream, French beans and carrots, and a side salad.

Alison told them about her visit to Jack. How he'd almost got moved that day, but his solicitor had halted it, and he would be going to a London jail tomorrow. Nova gave more details on the visit to Mrs Litt, her nervousness, her carelessness with a key under a pot. Then she got on to Tahir Ahmed, the fast and loose, now total boss of Litt & Ahmed. A definite suspect. She followed that with her chat with Sarah Raban, Litt's PA and mistress.

'She said he was an awful bully who screwed lots of people in his business dealing. She's sending me a list of people he crossed.'

'I hope it's not too long,' said Alison.

'It's why murder investigations have big teams,' said Nova, taking more French beans and carrots. 'What starts out simple, expands into lots of different areas, and you need 30 or more to cover them all. Not three part-timers.'

They concentrated on eating, a little overwhelmed by all that had to be done.

'That recording will likely help Jack,' said Alison, adding more sour cream to her potato, 'but it incriminates you, Nova.'

'I shall have to argue necessity. I'll take it into the station first thing in the morning. And hope I can swing it.'

'The gun,' said Mia. 'How can we find out who might have had it?'

'I have a contact,' said Nova, 'who might be able to help. The 7mm bullets, as I said, they are most likely from a

Penna 7mm. An Italian small arm. But my contact won't give me anything useful, me being a cop. I wondered if you could speak to him, Alison? Not on the phone. It'll have to be face to face.'

'Not exactly my field,' she said uncomfortably, 'but it's me or no one, I suppose.'

'Please,' pleaded Nova.

Mia had been listening quietly, feeling somewhat left out as the cop and her mother decided what had to be done. She had a thought of what she might do, somewhat dangerous, and bound to be vetoed by these two. So she kept it to herself.

Chapter 28

Jack was eating breakfast when an officer entered his cell with a large cardboard box.

'Pack your stuff in here,' he said. 'You're off to Pentonville in 40 minutes.'

A new cop, one he'd not seen before. He brusquely put down the box and left.

On the cell floor was his half completed jigsaw of The Haywain, so much cloud and sky. Pity to take it to bits with all that done. It had taken him much of the last evening to get so far.

This was his life, upset at having to take a jigsaw to pieces. It struck him, that was the truth of it; he had no control. He was a prisoner, admittedly one on remand, but at the beck and call of anonymous authorities. They housed him, woke him up, fed him, they transported him without notice.

Jack finished his breakfast: sausages, eggs and beans with toast and tea. They'd run out of Rice Crispies this morning. He'd been given cornflakes as an alternative, but had never liked cornflakes and left the little box unopened. The extent of his control and rebellion.

The food was fine, he had no complaints, apart from running out of Rice Crispies. He could write to his MP about that. Or maybe the King.

Pack. A two-minute job.

He should phone Alison and tell her he was going to Pentonville. Jack pressed the assistance buzzer and in a few minutes, the cop came back. Jack told him that he had to make a phone call. The officer nodded and went away. A little later, he returned with another officer.

Jack was handcuffed and taken to the custody sergeant's area. He was given a landline to make his call. He phoned Alison and told her he was about to be taken to Pentonville in half an hour. When she'd got that, he asked about the recording she'd mentioned on her visit yesterday. The one that would prove that he was not having an affair with Mrs Litt. Who was it with, what did it say?

Alison began explaining but he couldn't really understand what she was saying, something about a cat's tattoo on his thigh which he didn't have. So what was that about, and why did she think it helped him? He didn't feel able to delve deeper with the cops so close.

He closed the call and was taken back to his cell. Jack slumped on the bench in disappointment. He'd had some hopes on the recording but it didn't seem to be anything at all. Soon he'd be carted off to jail, where he'd be for the next year, while the court processes wound their uncaring way to his trial.

Jack had not moved when the cops came back. Irritated with him, they slung his things in the cardboard box, including the jigsaw pieces. They handcuffed him, gave him the untidy box to hold, jigsaw pieces on top of clothes, his book and old newspapers. The officers directed him out to the car park where the prison van was waiting.

Chapter 29

Nova had worked late last night after leaving Alison's. She had been at the station until almost midnight, finishing the paperwork that she hadn't touched during the day.

At least, she'd caught up.

She rose at seven. Important things to do today. And was back in the station by 8 am. Her boss Fayyad was already in. Without further todo, she played him the recording of her and Mrs Litt, which she now had on her laptop. She watched him as he listened, trying to glean his reaction. Having been so sure of its efficacy when she was with Mia and Alison, today she was unsure how well it stood up on its own, whether it could be read differently.

When it finished, he asked her whether Jack had a cat tattoo on his thigh. She told him he hadn't. Fayyad told her to replay the recording. And then for a third time.

'What do you think?' she said.

'The woman's a liar.' He picked up his desk phone and dialled.

'DI Kamani, ma'am. I have a recording I'd like you to listen to.'

In a few minutes, they were in Chief Superintendent Nikki Martin's office.

They sat down before her desk. Nova opened her laptop.

'Before I hear your recording,' said Martin, 'tell me how you got it?'

Nova knew she'd be asked this. She couldn't say she got in by pretending to be a replacement FLO. So keeping it simple was the plan.

'I went to see Mrs Litt.' She shrugged, to indicate how easy it had been. 'And I talked to her.'

Missing out the difficulty in getting in, the lies she'd had to tell.

'This is most unorthodox,' said Martin. 'You are getting yourself in the most awful hot water, DC Taylor. You cannot simply interview witnesses in another case.'

'Even if there's a miscarriage of justice, ma'am?'

Martin thought a while.

'Let's hear the recording, and then I'll see how it fits.'

Nova was gratified to get this far. She clicked, and tuned herself out as it played. She'd heard the little piece too many times to be able to listen any longer. When it finished, seeing Martin somewhat nonplussed, she explained Jack didn't have a tattoo, not of any sort.

'May I ask how you know that, DC Taylor?'

'I'm his girlfriend, ma'am.'

Martin smiled. 'That explains a lot. Play it again.'

Nova watched the Chief Superintendent as the file replayed. The Chief Superintendent had her eyes closed, listening intensely. Well, she was giving it a hearing. She crossed her fingers that it would stand up.

When the recording ended, Martin said, 'That is definitely Mrs Litt talking to you?'

'Yes, ma'am.'

'Obtained with subterfuge,' she said. 'Though I am sure you could not have got it any other way. What do you think, DI Kamani?'

'It's a damning piece of evidence, ma'am. The woman is a liar.'

Martin nodded. 'Let's get DI Hawley here.'

In a few minutes, Hawley joined them. She brought in a coffee in a paper cup. There were crumbs on her chin, suggesting she had been interrupted at breakfast.

Hawley was somewhat put out to see both Fayyad and Nova in the office.

'I have a complaint of gross misconduct against DC Taylor, ma'am,' she said.

'So you have,' said Martin. 'And you may well have more complaints in a little while.' She turned to Nova. 'Play the first bit of the recording. I'll tell you when to stop.'

Nova clicked the file. She knew what Martin was doing: getting the voices before the meat of the interview. Smart.

'Stop,' exclaimed Martin after less than half a minute. To Hawley, she said, 'Do you recognise the voices?'

'Yes,' she said, 'it's DC Taylor talking to Yvonne Litt. I don't understand, what's this all about?' She turned on Nova. 'How did you make that recording, Taylor?'

'Before we get into the whys and wherefores,' said Martin, 'listen to it all first. Play it from the beginning, DC Taylor.'

Nova offered DI Hawley her seat. She refused, not wanting to accept anything from the reprobate. Nova played the recording and watched Hawley. She had a frown that became more pronounced as the recording went on. By the end she was shaking her head.

'This is preposterous,' she exclaimed. 'This pipsqueak is doing all she can to undermine my case. Do you know, ma'am, she is the girlfriend of Jack Bell?'

'I have been told,' said Martin.

'And I'm not sure it is Yvonne Litt speaking.'

'You said it was,' retorted Nova.

'Voices can be imitated. Faked.'

'You are so one-sided!' declared Nova. 'You dismiss anything that doesn't fit.'

'How dare you speak that way to a superior officer!'

'At police college, I was told to believe the evidence and not your prejudices.'

'Listen, Little Miss Detective.' Hawley pushed her face close to Nova's. 'You have been in this game for five minutes. You have a complaint against you of gross misconduct. Whereas I am a Detective Inspector with more than ten years experience. I have cleared up more murders than you have had hot dinners!'

'But you won't accept evidence that challenges your case!'

'Enough, DC Taylor!' exclaimed Martin. 'It is obvious that the two of you are on opposite sides of the fence.'

'Mrs Litt is a liar!' declared Nova. 'Doesn't the recording make that clear?'

She turned to them all. It was so obvious to her.

'Your lover is charged with murder,' said Hawley, resting a hand on Nova's shoulder, which Nova shook off. 'And you will stop at nothing to get him off. But I tell you this, you greenhorn, there's blood in his van, and no recording will alter that.'

'Planted!' she yelled.

Martin threw up her hands in exasperation. 'Enough, both of you.' She turned to Nova. 'I expect more respect from you to a superior officer.'

'Yes, ma'am.'

She wanted to keep the Chief Inspector on her side. She couldn't care less about Hawley, who was stupid and bigoted.

Martin turned to Hawley.

'This is evidence,' she said. 'I expect you to treat it as such.'

'Does that mean Jack is released?' said Nova.

Hawley laughed. 'See how she works to undermine my case!'

'It means,' said Martin, 'that we will bring Mrs Litt in. I want you, DI Kamani, to go and arrest her with your maddening assistant. And I want you, DI Hawley, to stay here. We will review the evidence and speak to the Crime Prosecution Service.'

Chapter 30

Mia went up the path. By the door of the house, looking about to see if anyone was watching, she tipped the large urn. From under it, she saw the key, just where Nova said it was. She put it in the lock of the front door and opened it. She slipped into the house and quietly closed the door behind her.

A wide hallway was in front of her, about halfway along there were stairs going up. She had no idea where she should go or what she was looking for. Just a vague thought there might be something incriminating somewhere.

She'd thought about what to wear for her mission. Nothing outrageous, settling for jeans and a plain green t-shirt, no slogan to make her memorable. She had crowded her hair into a grey, nondescript beanie, trainers on her feet if she needed to do a runner.

The hallway had no hiding places. Mia crept down it, stopping at the foot of the stairs. Should she stay down here or try upstairs? But all the rooms up there, anyone could be in them. And did it really matter where she started searching for the vital piece of evidence?

Whatever it was.

She needed to show them. Her mum especially, always lecturing her on what to wear, how to behave, telling her she should be studying and not marching to save the planet. And Nova too, she might be the detective, but she, Mia, would come up with something, a vital piece of evidence. And they'd all say, Aha! That's brilliant, Mia. We'd never have found it in a month of Sundays.

At home, before she headed off on her adventure, her mother had had a phone call from her father. They were taking him to Pentonville. Mia didn't know where it was, but recalled a blue square on the Monopoly board. Her mother told her it was in Islington, and said it could've been a lot worse.

There was a voice from a room down the hallway. She crept that way, and came to the open door of a large kitchen. There were some units and a cooker. What she couldn't see was the speaker. A woman, probably Mrs Litt. The liar.

'My iPhone isn't working,' said the woman, obviously speaking on a phone, presumably her landline. 'I don't know why. I just can't get into it. It asks me for touch ID, and then won't accept it. It's broken.'

No it isn't, thought Mia, chuffed at the woman's frustration. It's not yours.

'How can they know that?' exclaimed Mrs Litt. A pause. 'It must've been that woman who came. Said she was family liaison. I can't remember her name.' A pause. 'Yes, blonde hair in a ponytail.' A pause. 'They are coming here for me?' A pause. 'Well, I'd better get a move on. See you in half an hour.'

Suddenly Mia could see her, coming for the kitchen door. A tall slim woman with hair to her shoulders, in jeans and a white t-shirt, the one for the festival with the Forest Gate clock in the centre. She had one herself.

'Who the hell are you?' exclaimed Mrs Litt, brought up short at seeing the intruder.

Mia was taken aback by the encounter. But she could see that the woman was more disturbed than she was. And what could she do? Mia took a deep breath.

'I am a private detective,' she said.

'You can't just break into houses.' Mrs Litt was shaking, flustered. 'That's a crime.'

'And so is murder,' said Mia.

'Who are you?' There was terror in her face.

'You are Mrs Litt,' said Mia, ignoring her question, 'and you are part of a criminal conspiracy to frame Jack Bell.'

Mrs Litt looked wildly about her, almost collapsing against the wall.

'How do you know?' she said weakly.

'I am employed by Jack Bell. We have your phone.'

'No, you don't.' She showed the one she was holding.

'That's not yours. Which is why you can't get in.' She put her hand out. 'It was switched.'

'The woman who came yesterday...' Mrs Litt was almost sliding down the wall. 'The so-called family liaison officer.'

'Let me have the phone.' Mia held out her hand. 'It's no good to you.'

Mrs Litt threw it down the hallway.

'I shall call the police on you,' she exclaimed. 'You are a burglar.'

'I haven't stolen anything,' said Mia, though she could have added 'yet', as theft was her intention. 'But do phone the police, Mrs Litt. It will save time.'

Knowing she wouldn't.

Mia went down the hallway and picked up the phone. The glass was cracked. They charged a fortune to replace it. She returned to the sagging heap that was Mrs Litt.

'We know,' said Mia, standing over her, fully in command, 'there was no affair between you and my client.'

'How do you know?'

'That nonsense about the cat tattoo. The conversation was recorded. Mr Bell has no tattoo on his thigh, or anywhere else.'

Mrs Litt smiled weakly. 'I should have known it was a trick.'

'Who is your accomplice?' said Mia.

'I'll take you to her.' She rose, pressing against the wall to support herself. 'Yes, it will all be explained. You'll see how it happened. All an accident. Please come with me.' She looked at her watch. 'I've got to get out of here. Come along. It will all be explained. What's your name?'

'Nancy,' said Mia, nearly adding Drew.

'We must go, Nancy. I'll explain on the way.'

She ushered Mia along the hallway, out of the front door, and into her car.

Chapter 31

Fayyad was driving, with Nova beside him in the passenger's seat. Traffic on the Romford Road was busy. It would have been quicker to walk, but they were picking up Mrs Litt, and a car made it more official. And more discreet, if they had to use handcuffs.

'You didn't say anything in the Chief's office,' said Nova.

'You didn't need me,' said Fayyad with a laugh. 'You were doing very well on your own.'

'DI Hawley hates me like poison.'

'She doesn't like being thwarted.' He halted in a line of vehicles at the traffic lights. 'Better, I thought, if I shut up, then I can speak to her Inspector to Inspector. Whereas you have blown any hope of a polite chat with her.'

'I'd like to be a fly on the wall while she was with the Chief.'

'Hawley will be calling you an interfering nobody. She'll be trying to downgrade the recording. And the Chief will be telling her it is evidence. Not evidence she can ignore. Too many people know about it.'

'It cracks her case wide open,' said Nova. 'Shows she's been barking up the wrong tree.' She sighed. 'I was hoping the Chief would order Jack's release.'

'She can't. He's been to magistrate's court, CPS would have to give the say-so. And there's still the matter of blood in his van...'

'But just the blood. And a liar. It spells frame-up clear as day.'

'He's been taken to Pentonville. I saw him being led out to the van carrying a big cardboard box.' He laughed. 'I picked up one of his jigsaw pieces in the hallway. A piece of cloudy sky. I wonder how I can get that to him.'

Nova didn't reply, reckoning a piece of sky was the least of Jack's troubles. Pentonville. She wondered how he would get on there, amongst all the hard men.

They turned into Woodgrange High Street. The traffic was sluggish this morning, they were stuck behind a bus.

'Mrs Litt has a lot of explaining to do,' said Fayyad. 'And I don't want to leave her interview to Hawley.'

'She lied about having an affair with Jack. But she has an alibi for the night. She was at the theatre...'

'But she hasn't one for the day,' said Fayyad, 'when the murder was committed.'

'You've been looking at Holmes!' exclaimed Nova.

'I have to keep up with my maddening assistant.' He halted the car in the middle of the road, to turn right into Hampton Road. 'If we accept she wasn't on the Flats depositing the body, then it's obvious there's more than one person involved.'

They turned into Hampton Road.

'There! There!' exclaimed Nova, pointing. 'That's Mia and Mrs Litt in that car.'

They had just turned into the road, and Mrs Litt's car was at the top of the road, parallel with them, waiting for the traffic to clear and let them onto the main road.

Fayyad braked.

Nova leapt out of the car, raced a few yards, and stood in front of Mrs Litt's vehicle.

'Turn off the engine!' she yelled to the terrified driver through the windscreen, arms wide across the car bonnet.

Mia gave a brief wave to Nova, leaned over Mrs Litt and turned off the engine.

Fayyad was out of his car. He crossed the road and stood by the window of their quarry. He opened her car door.

'Are you Mrs Yvonne Litt?'

'I am,' came the timid reply.

'She is for sure,' added Mia, to make certain he knew absolutely.

Fayyad nodded at her, and gave the official caution to Mrs Litt.

'Yvonne Litt, I am arresting you as an accomplice in the murder of Tom Litt. You do not have to say anything. But it may harm your defence if you do not mention when questioned something which you later rely on in court. Anything you do say may be given in evidence.'

Her head sank onto the steering wheel.

Chapter 32

There had been six stalls in the van. None could see each other but they could speak. Some were silent, he had nothing himself to add to the general talk. Two inmates spoke about Pentonville, where they were all going, and comparing it with other jails. Worse than some, better than others. One prisoner was dying for a pee, as the vehicle had been to six police stations picking up prisoners. 'I'm going to pee myself if you don't let me out!'

They didn't let him out. From which Jack gathered that if he was ever driven to another jail, keep liquid consumption beforehand to a minimum. Knowledge he hoped he would never need, but he had no say in his recent travel plans. He had almost been taken to Parkhurst on the Isle of Wight, prevented only by his solicitor. Which reminded him, he must contact her to say where he was. Or did the police inform her?

On arrival at Pentonville, the van went through gate after gate, before stopping in the inner car park. They all alighted and he saw his fellow prisoners for the first time, all handcuffed, and one with liquid stains down his trousers.

Jack's box was taken away. It would be returned to him, he was informed, once it had been shown to be clear of contraband. Drugs, phones, he assumed. The next couple of hours consisted of form-filling. A few by him, but mostly in conjunction with various prison officials. He hadn't realised it was so hard to get into jail. They wanted to know about his education (or lack of), his health, his next of kin (he gave Mia and his mother, who didn't yet know he was in prison), his religion (or lack of), his diet and his sexual orientation.

He was strip searched, which consisted of taking all his clothes off and sitting on an odd chair which enabled an officer to peer into his anus. That really showed him his place.

Jack's picture was taken and he was given an identity card with his photo and prisoner number. He was told not to lose it as it would be a hassle to get a new one, and he would need it for just about everything inside. He signed numerous forms too quickly, some he barely understood. A prison officer asked him whether he smoked. He thought of saying that he did, as the little he knew of prison told him that tobacco was currency, and he noted that those who said they were smokers were given a smoker's pack. But he decided against it, and was given a small carton of orange juice and a small pack of biscuits.

The form-filling done, he was handed on to an inmate, who was disappointed Jack had no cigarettes. But once the inmate was over his chagrin, he answered Jack's questions about phone calls, visits, washing, meals, exercise and violence in the prison. And rules and rules.

The place was confusingly big, with so many keys, filled with dangerous men. So maybe the rules were needed to stop them killing each other in a mad spree.

Several hours after his arrival, Jack was at last taken to a cell along a corridor of cells. He had been given sheets, blankets, a pillow, a plastic plate, a mug and cutlery along with a washing pack and some prison clothing. He thought it best to accept the latter, although being on remand he was allowed his own clothes, but they might be some time coming. He'd already got the feeling that there was no rush in here, he was just one of many numbers in a vast warren of numbers. Whether he would ever see the cardboard box which had his clothing and the jigsaw amongst the other items, as well as that book Alison had given him, was anyone's guess.Jack wasn't alone in the cell. He had been locked in with another new inmate who grabbed the top bunk, leaving Jack the bottom one. There was a toilet in the cell with a flimsy curtain round it. In this small space, they'd get to know each other pretty well, from toilet habits to love life, no doubt with lots of lies and excuses thrown in.

What was his companion in for? Fraud, burglary or murder? Jack would have to get on with him, no matter what.

Chapter 33

DI Fayyad Kamani and DI Kate Hawley were in the office of their Chief, Nikki Martin. She was exasperated with the pair of them.

'It is my case!' declared Hawley.

She had a coffee with her, there were rings round her eyes that she'd tried to disguise with make-up. The case was wearing her out, thought Fayyad. She's hitting out. He had crossed with her before, she would never admit to making a mistake.

He had tried reasoning with her, but it didn't work. Even less did shouting, but that's where they had got to.

'You had her one hundred percent wrong,' said Fayyad. 'Mrs Litt was your chief witness. DC Taylor has proved her to be a liar, which had you stomping around like an elephant on steroids.' He turned to his Chief. 'So how can she now interview her?'

Nikki Martin pressed two hands on her desk. Leaning forward, she said, 'Let's have some hush, and let me consider the best course of action. I acknowledge it is your case, DI Hawley, but you must acknowledge that Mrs Litt is lying.'

'Only if the recording is a true recording.'

'See! See!' interjected Fayyad, 'nothing will make her change her mind.'

'You said it sounds like Mrs Litt,' said Martin.

'Yes, it does, but that doesn't make the recording genuine.'

Martin turned to Fayyad. 'Why do you think it is a true recording, DI Kamani?'

'Because DC Taylor says it is, and having worked with her for a year, I trust her. Besides which, she would have had to employ an actor. Found one with the right voice, done a lot of auditions...' He threw his hands out. 'When would she have time or the skills for that?'

'She will do anything to get her lover out of jail!'exclaimed Hawley, banging the desk with her fist.

'Enough!' Martin put out her hands to foreclose any more comments. 'We are going round in circles. There is only one thing for it; I suggest you both interview her.'

'That's preposterous,' exclaimed Hawley.

'If it's too preposterous for you,' said Martin, 'You can watch the interview on screen.'

Hawley was about to speak, but bit the words back.

'How do we do it?' said Fayyad.

'You take it in turns to question her. No follow-ups.'

'Could be clumsy,' said Fayyad.

'Got any better ideas?'

He shrugged. He hadn't. But he didn't like it. You had to have interviewers in agreement on tactics, not fighting like stags in rut.

Martin took out a coin. She spun it in the air and caught it.

'Heads or tails,' she said to Hawley.

'Heads.'

Martin opened her hand. 'Heads it is. You start. But both remember, the object is not to score points, but to get to the truth, even if that messes up prior ideas.'

Chapter 34

Jack's box had arrived. It was surprisingly comforting. It meant Pentonville jail wasn't total chaos, there was some method in all the corridors, keys and form filling. The bits and pieces in the box gave him identity, as stupid and as little as that was. The clothing, old newspapers, his astronomy mag, the jigsaw puzzle and the book Alison had given him, Are We Alone in the Universe, they proved he was who he was.

As he went through the items, he realised how much reassurance we need. He was Jack Bell, builder, father, lover, amateur astronomer, with a life in Forest Gate. Take the reassurance away, as ruthless dictators did by throwing critics into solitary confinement. In a bare cell, the minimum of food, no visitors, lies from jailers, nothing to read, no sense of time, how soon anyone would disintegrate.

He must write letters, read, talk in order to stay sane. He had a case to fight, or rather those outside, whom he had absolute reliance on, were fighting for him. He hoped. He needed to talk to Alison and his solicitor, to find out what was going on.

That could drive you crackers too. The helplessness. Being shut in, not knowing what, if anything was being done for you.

The walls don't speak.

Jack had not said a word to his companion, who was in the top bunk. Half asleep, silently weeping, or daydreaming of freedom on a beach in Spain.

'Do you like jigsaws?' he said.

His companion sat up. He was almost bald, his head shaved, in his mid-50s, on the fat side. His teeth appeared in good shape but would later be revealed as mostly dentures. He was wearing a light grey loose top and bottoms, the shapeless tracksuit the prison provided as standard wear.

'Might as well.'

He came down the short ladder attached to the bunks. At ground level, he hitched up his bottoms, the elastic on its last legs, and stared at the pieces Jack had poured onto the floor.

'We got plenty of time for this,' he said, getting down to Jack's level. 'Seven years, me. How about you, mate?'

They had begun turning over the many pieces to show snippets of the picture, and spreading them out.

'I'm on remand,' said Jack.

'What for?'

'Murder.'

What a reply, Jack thought as he said it. He wondered how it sounded, and thought of adding he was innocent, but everyone said that, and maybe it was better to sound like a hard man.

'And you?' he said.

The man was sorting out pieces of sky and cloud.

'Rape,' he said.

Jack was under no illusion he was locked in with angels. And to prove it, here was a rapist who had been sentenced to seven years. He would ask no more, as he knew he had to get on with the man, no matter what was his wickedness. Any arguments in this small lock-up and they could kill each other.

Though rape took some processing. In some other setting, he'd have Googled the man, got the details of the case. Seven years was no joke. It must have been a violent attack. Weird to watch him picking over jigsaw pieces. He could have been a favourite uncle by the Christmas tree.

'Let me do the sky and clouds,' said the man. 'You do the river and stuff.'

That was fine by Jack. Relieved the man was getting into the jigsaw. Jack watched his busyness. He was sorting out the edge pieces. The man had done a lot of jigsaws, which suggested he'd been in jail before, maybe repeatedly.

'Jack.' He held out his hand.

'Bic. Like the pen.'

They shook hands over the pieces.

Prison, he'd begun to realise, was about getting used to new situations, some dangerous. He'd been flung into a cell with a stranger, a rapist, he now knew as Bic who liked jigsaws. Who'd probably been as wary of him as he was of Bic. Or more so, as Jack was a murderer, the lack of detail adding to his aura.

Oh, hard man of Pentonville.

The relief was tremendous. They'd bonded over a jigsaw.

Chapter 35

Hawley and Fayyad were on one side of the table in the interview room. Mrs Litt and the duty solicitor on the other. She had been weeping, her face stained with tears. Her white t-shirt was grubby, the design, a celebration of Forest Gate Festival, somewhat out of keeping in this utterly functional room.

He and Hawley had had an awkward chat before coming into the room. They had agreed they were not to argue during the interview, but rather to back each other up. If there was any point of contention, either could call a temporary halt to sort out the problem.

He knew what Hawley was after. It didn't need the wisdom of Solomon; she didn't want her key witness destroyed. What a game, manipulating truth, making new truths. She was maintaining that the recording was a fake, made by Nova to free her lover. Fayyad found that quite ridiculous. All the trouble she would have to go to, finding someone who sounded like Mrs Litt and then coaching her. She would have had to write a script for her actor!

But that's what Hawley was pushing. In her eyes, Jack and Mrs Litt were lovers, she wanted the jury to accept that. If that trope was discredited, her case began to disintegrate.

Did she really believe it, or was it a result at any cost? Or maybe some amalgam of the two, she believed it because it would work for her. And to backtrack, to admit a mistake, wasn't in her lexicon.

Having witnessed how she worked close up, Fayyad wondered about her other cases. Was it always a result at any cost?

Some other time he'd burrow into that. Now he must get what he could out of the interview. The cat-and-mouse interview technique wasn't satisfactory. He going for one scenario, Hawley for another, it would make them a weak team. She hadn't wanted him here at all, for obvious reasons. But he'd argued his way in with the Chief. And now in the seat, he would do what he could to get to the truth of the matter.

Mrs Litt was definitely shaky. She'd spent a couple of hours in a cell before coming up for the interview, and was most unhappy. The grubby t-shirt, the tear-stained face, she could at least have had a wash but had given up on her appearance. So maybe, in her state of despair, she'd begin to sing.

The duty solicitor was by her side, a reliable old hand. He'd look after her interests. Fayyad had the uncomfortable feeling that Hawley would too.

The tape and video recorder were started. DI Hawley said who was present, and gave time and date. The duty solicitor was Peter Stone, the one who had assisted Jack in his first interview. It seemed he was a regular.

Mrs Litt was asked to confirm her name and where she lived. She did so. Non-contentious stuff to confirm her identity.

'You are the widow of Tom Litt?' said Hawley.

'I am,' she said.

Hardly deniable. It was why they were here.

Mrs Litt was not handcuffed. They would have no trouble handling her if she got violent, though her submissive demeanour suggested that was most unlikely.

'I am going to play you a recording,' said Fayyad. It was his throw of the dice. This was the big one.

He clicked the file and watched her intently as the recording played. Her face was twitchy, several times she took a sharp intake of breath. She'd known of the existence of the recording, Mia playing detective had told her, but she had not heard it. He saw her wincing, as she heard herself trying to explain the cat tattoo. Nova's fiction.

The recording ended.

Fayyad said, 'Is that you in the recording, Mrs Litt?'

'No comment,' she said.

A not-unexpected reply, though a pity, as it meant it would have to be proved that it was her voice in the recording, and proving such things always left room for doubt.

'Were you involved in the killing of your husband?' said Hawley.

'No.'

Fayyad left to his own devices would not have asked that question, at least not yet, but he had to go along with his fellow interviewer.

'Were you having an affair with Jack Bell?' he said.

She hesitated for a second before answering.

'No comment.'

Not helpful, as she could have hesitated because she didn't want to admit to an affair or alternatively, because she had lied saying they'd been having one. All good fun for the lawyers.

'In your statement,' said Hawley, 'you said you and Jack Bell became lovers early in his employment. Is that true?'

Hawley badly wanted a yes on that, so she was trying again, referring Mrs Litt to her statement.

'No comment.'

Make what you will of that, thought Fayyad. Not backing up her own statement was at least a sign of confusion. Quite who that assisted was arguable.

'Does Jack Bell have a cat's head tattoo on his thigh?' he said.

'No comment.'

His heart sank. It was going to be one of those interviews. Quite fruitless. Mrs Litt would say 'no comment' to anything contentious. Her right, of course.

'Where were you on Monday evening?' asked Hawley.

'I was at the National Theatre with my friend Mary Trott. I didn't get home till after 11pm. We saw Cat on a Hot Tin Roof.'

Not on a hot thigh, thought Fayyad.

It was accepted she had been at the theatre. Mary Trott had been interviewed and said she had been Mrs Litt's companion, and had the ticket stubs and programme. So Mrs Litt couldn't have been out on the Flats that night when Jack found the body.

But the body had been dead for many hours, so the theatre was just half an alibi.

'I put it to you, Mrs Litt,' said Fayyad, 'that you were an accomplice in your husband's murder. Your role was to say you were having an affair with Jack Bell, who is now in Pentonville Jail, on your say-so, on a charge of murder.'

Hawley trod on his foot. Clearly, she didn't like the question.

'I, we...' stammered Mrs Litt, 'never meant to...'

Peter Stone intervened. 'I would like to talk to my client.'

This was allowable. Recording and video were halted, Fayyad and Hawley left the room while Stone talked to his client.

He and Hawley were in the corridor, outside the interview room. It was obvious what Stone was saying to Mrs Litt. Shut up – or you will go to jail for obstruction of justice. Or even worse – being an accomplice to murder.

'That was an underhand question,' hissed Hawley.

'It was a perfectly good question,' he said. 'She started to admit something, for heaven's sake. What are we here for? To get her to tell the truth, surely?'

'Not to browbeat a vulnerable witness.'

He harrumphed at her sympathy.

'She said: I, we never meant to...' said Fayyad. 'That says to me, she was working with someone, and she never meant Jack to go down for murder.'

'It's a lot to hang on those few words.'

'Take the 'we',' he said, 'what do you make of it then?'

She didn't reply, but he could feel her hostility. If the duty solicitor hadn't been with Mrs Litt, and hadn't been so quick off the mark, she would have revealed so much more. At this very moment, the solicitor would be telling her that she must not incriminate herself.

And bang would go the rest of the interview.

Which proved to be true. When the interview recommenced, Mrs Litt said 'No Comment' to everything asked of her. A boring, tedious sequence, which they called a day after 12 questions resulting in the same non-answer.

She had been well advised.

It all came down to what a jury would make of 'I, we, never meant to...'. To Fayyad the 'we' suggested conspiracy, with at least one other person involved, and 'never meant to' said to him that she didn't want Jack done for murder.

He was biased but, surely, another hole had been made in Hawley's case.

Chapter 36

Alison was in an estate agent's in Canning Town. The area had changed considerably in thirty years, from a deprived, undesirable area, in middle class terms, to one more desirable, though the deprivation remained, surrounding the estates of incoming home owners.

This estate agent was a symbol of the change.

She was seated across from a young woman, who no doubt thought Alison a potential house buyer. In her tweed dress suit, Alison had come straight from school, she was the epitome of middle class affluence.

'What are you looking for, madam?' said the young woman, trying to smooth away the local accent. Her blonde hair was tied back in a ponytail. She wore a white shirt and a navy blue pleated skirt, as did two other women. The uniform. They could have been sixth formers; they were hardly much older.

The large office was bland. Its front window was full of houses and flats on offer, while inside the three women sat at well-spaced desks. There was a fridge, with a glass door, packed with bottles of fruit juice and water. At the rear was a glass-walled office; the boss, she surmised. The furniture was new, standard office, with a few large, black and white photos of old Canning Town on the walls, to give the space a little gravitas. But it didn't work. This was a selling hall.

'I want to speak to Ethan Allen,' said Alison.

A flicker of disappointment crossed the woman's face. Here was no commission.

'May I ask what for?'

'No.'

You don't confide to a young estate agent that you have come to discuss an illegal gun.

The woman looked uncomfortably to the glass office at the rear, where a man was on the phone.

'I'm afraid Mr Allen is busy at the moment. Would you like to make an appointment?'

'No,' said Alison.

She rose and walked to the glass office.

'Madam, you can't...' the young woman called after her in alarm.

But Alison pushed open the door of the hallowed space. She sat herself down in front of the desk. There had been no point talking further with the young woman. She was a barrier, and direct action was the only alternative to leaving.

The man, still on the phone, looked at her in some annoyance. He was in a smart grey suit, a pale blue shirt with what appeared to be a regimental tie. He was late 30s, early 40s, his hair too black, beginning to go grey she knew, as she was hitting that herself, but using less obvious hair colouring. The man was stocky; she felt a muscular aggression, not typical estate agent fare.

There was a laptop on the desk, and music was playing from the sound system on the shelving behind him. She caught the lyrics, doe, a deer, a female deer, before he turned it off.

The office was pleasantly air-conditioned. Which wasn't any help as she had come in uninvited to ask awkward questions.

'Talk to you later,' said the man on the phone. 'I've got an awkward customer.'

She waited. She was trespassing. The young woman outside was signalling that she couldn't stop the intrusion. He waved her away.

'Who the hell are you?' he said, in a very East End accent.

'Alison Bell, principal of Cumberland Primary School in Hackney.'

He dismissed her with a flick of his hand.

'We only give to local charities.'

'I've come to talk about a gun, Mr Allen, a Penna, 7mm. I have been told you might be able to assist.'

He sat up straight in his chair, suddenly in business mode.

'This is an estate agent, madam.' He indicated about him. 'As you can see.'

She had expected this. You don't tell all and sundry your illegal business.

'DC Taylor said you would help me.'

The man looked thoughtful, rubbing his chin, looking her up and down, assessing her utility and sexuality. He was a dangerous man, she could feel it, that predatory searching. The estate agency, legitimate in its way, was a front to other businesses. More lucrative.

What areas did it cover? Alison wasn't particularly knowledgeable about crime, but it took no insider intelligence to be aware that guns had a major role in drugs gangs, robberies and prostitution.

'DC Taylor said the Forest Gate shooting...' said Alison, 'she says if you assist in this, she'll keep you out of it.'

Nova had told her it was believed that Ethan Allen had likely supplied the gun in the Forest Gate shooting. She'd said it was better to use him than arrest him. Though this could easily change.

'You wired?' he said.

'No.' She was familiar enough with US cop shows to know the meaning.

He thought for a few seconds, his face twisting in assessing how much he could say or offer.

'Come with me,' he said.

He led her into a windowless side room. There were stacks of cardboard boxes filling much of the space. An open one was full of housing literature.

'Stay here. I'll be back in a mo'.

He left the room, closing the door on her. It clicked shut. Was she locked in? She went to the door and tried the handle. She was. Had she walked into a trap? He would come back with his henchmen; they'd beat her up, torture and strip her. She'd end up floating in the River Lea.

She shivered. What had she walked into? She could be raped, gang raped, electricity connected to her privates, until she had admitted every crime going, any time and any place. Yes, she had killed Kennedy, she had organised the planes crashing into the twin towers, she had sold nuclear secrets to the Chinese, the Russians, the Saudi Arabians. Ask her and she would confess.

She was defenceless, a total coward, utterly stupefied.

There was a single bare light bulb in the middle of the ceiling. Alison looked around the airless, windowless space and wondered how many people had been tortured here. The only way out was through his office. Her phone had no signal. He was in total control.

She sat on a box, her knee trembling. There was no furniture. She mustn't fall to bits. Must at least act confident. She breathed in and out, concentrating on her breathing, on the dust in the air, on the lightbulb and the silence in this muffled room.

The door opened.

The man entered with the young woman she had first talked to, with the blonde ponytail. Alison was relieved to see them, but aware that might be premature.

'Search her for a wire, Moira.'

'Sorry, madam,' said Moira, 'but I have to be a little intimate. Please stand up.'

Not quite so polite as in their first encounter. Alison stood up.

Moira frisked her up and down in the obvious and less obvious places, while the man looked on with a wry smile as his assistant did the business.

'She's clean,' said Moira, 'and not recording anything on her phone.'

'Thank you, love. Leave us.'

Moira left, closing the door behind her. Alison fought off a sneeze in the dusty air.

'What's the gun again?'

'A Penna 7mm,' she said. Easy to remember, it made her think of pasta.

'That's unusual.'

'It's why we thought you could help.'

'So tell me why you want to know about it.'

She took a deep breath, and wished she hadn't in the fuggy atmosphere.

'My ex-husband is Jack Bell who...'

'Jack Bell, the builder?' exclaimed the man.

'Yes, that's him.'

'I went to school with him. Down Regency Lane. Well, well. Did some work for me a couple of years back. Good guy. Small world, eh?'

The mood was lightening. She shouldn't have been surprised at the breadth of Jack's acquaintances. He had lived in the borough all his life. Home, school, the streets, building work, there were a lot of people he'd rubbed shoulders with.

'Do you know Fayyad Kamani?' she said, endeavouring to use what she knew of Jack's friends, to lift the mood further.

And not be beaten senseless and tossed in the River Lea. In future, she would stick to governors' meetings and addressing the school at assembly. Not entering the lairs of East End gangsters.

'Fayyad! Course I do. Nice guy. A copper, though. A good cricketer, not my game. Jack Bell was OK at football, and not a bad builder.' He smiled, some friendliness in it, she felt with utter relief. 'Where's the gun come into it?'

'Jack is in Pentonville charged with murder.' Adding hastily, 'But he didn't do it.'

'They all say that.'

'It's true. The victim Tom Litt...'

151

'That bastard!' he interrupted, 'I'd have shot him myself ten times over.' He punched into his palm. 'Nice one, Jack.'

'He didn't do it, Mr Allen,' she said patiently. 'Ballistics reckon the bullets came from a Penna 7mm. We want to know who had it.'

'I get the picture, Alison. If I may call you that. A school principal, eh?'

'I was married to Jack for ten years.'

She didn't want to get into the history of why she no longer was.

'He's not a murderer,' she added. 'Please help, Mr Allen, or he could go down for 30 years.'

She left 20 minutes later with three names, and drove swiftly back to school. Never so pleased to be breathing the air of the law-abiding.

Chapter 37

Nova was in a small interview room. Not one for formal interviews for criminal cases, but for the many reasons that privacy is needed in a police station. Talking to witnesses or victims, taking statements, and in this instance, Nova was with an assessor for the complaint against her for gross misconduct.

Her assessor was Mr Bird, a black man in his late 20s. He had given up on his lack of hair and shaved his dome to a polished curvature. He wore black-rimmed glasses, giving him a severe expression. Bird was slim, in a grey, smart suit. He was not a cop, but an assessor of cops and not popular in the station. She wondered how you got that sort of job, and what it was like going daily into places where you are disliked.

'I am here,' explained Mr Bird, 'to give the Panel a first assessment in the case against you of gross misconduct. This is not a recorded interview. I shall take notes.' He had a notebook and a file of papers on the table before him. 'You have declined a Fed rep for this interview, DC Taylor.'

'I'll save my rep for the big day,' she said.

He shrugged. 'Your choice.' He glanced at his papers. 'The essence of the charge is that you, a detective constable, went to see your lover, who was imprisoned here and charged with murder. You were not working on his case, and improperly spoke to him about the case.' He looked up from his papers. 'Is that a fair assessment?'

'I'd rather not be called his lover, sir. That sounds like an illicit relationship. We are both single. Can we say girlfriend?'

'Point taken.'

'And yes, I went to see him. I don't dispute that. I thought the charge against him a major mistake. Jack Bell is not a murderer.'

'You are somewhat biased, DC Taylor.'

'He is not a murderer, sir,' Nova insisted. 'I went to see him, you might say as a girlfriend, but in the main to offer support to what I could see was a miscarriage of justice.'

'Outside your remit.'

'Is a miscarriage of justice outside anyone's remit?'

Bird wrote some rapid notes. She could read upside down usually, but not his squeezed hand. Perhaps he practised it on purpose.

'DI Hawley maintains that by talking to Bell,' said Bird, 'you informed him how the case was progressing, and you have undermined her case against him.'

'Firstly, I didn't tell Jack anything he didn't already know. And secondly, if I have undermined her case, then three cheers for it. It's all based on planted evidence and the lies of one woman, Mrs Litt, the widow of the victim.'

'A detective must not involve herself in other cases.'

'I did, I admit it. Throw me in the clink for attempting to right a miscarriage of justice.'

'No one is talking about jailing you.'

'Just drumming me out of the police force.'

Nova was feeling sticky round the collar in her fervour, too aware of the old saying, that an unrepresented defendant has a fool for a client. She felt she was striking wildly instead of concentrating on the major points.

'Suppose Jack Bell is innocent,' she said. 'Suppose DI Hawley has been barking up the wrong tree and has to be pulled back... Would that make my actions justifiable?'

'Is that the essence of your defence?' said Bird, looking at her quizzically.

'It's the basis, sir,' she said. She paused, gathering her resources. 'She is making a major error, and I can prove it. Will you talk to the Chief?'

'Why?'

'There's a recording which I intend using in my defence. It proves Mrs Litt is a liar.'

'You'll be using it in your defence, you say?'

'I most surely will. It proves the case against Jack Bell is fabricated and that...

Bird held up a hand. 'Stop there, DC Taylor. No point going over old ground. But if the recording is part of your defence, then I must hear it. I'll pay a visit to Chief Superintendent Martin and find out if it is pertinent. Don't go anywhere. I'll be back to finish the assessment as soon as I can.'

He left her, taking his notebook. His papers remained on the table, but she knew the contents: the charge against her, her defence and DI Hawley's reasons for the charge of gross misconduct. She had read it too many times.

Alone in the room, Nova took a deep breath and threw her head back. So difficult to know how Bird was reacting to her defence. She had seen no signs of sympathy. No doubt, you get pretty tough listening to special pleading. He'd be a stickler for the rules, a bible full of them, with clauses and sub clauses; who could not fall foul of them?

But this wasn't the Panel. Bird might be against her, but he wasn't the final judge. This was a first assessment. She'd at least get another chance if she failed this hurdle. Though it would be a bad sign.

She felt sick. Had she made things worse for herself by getting that recording? Doing even more of the forbidden, making it more certain she was on her last days as a copper.

All for Jack. But what else could she have done? She wasn't simply a copper, she was a girlfriend to a man in trouble.

She wondered what the Chief was saying to Bird. How she was angling it.

The phone in her pocket vibrated.

It was an email from Alison, who was obviously back in school as this was a lengthy message. She only sent short ones on her phone. Alison began by vehemently saying she was never ever going to see an East End gangster about a gun. She had never been so terrified in her life, realising how defenceless she was. He had locked her in a stock room. Fortunately, Ethan Allen turned out to be a schoolmate of Jack's, and DI Kamani for that matter. Saving her from being cut into kebab-size chunks and dumped in the River Lea. The upside was that she was still alive and had been given three names that the type of gun had gone to recently.

Alison added the names to the message. Two of them Nova didn't know. One, she most certainly did.

She made a call to Fayyad, asking if he could come down, as she was stuck in this room while the assessor spoke to the Chief. In a few minutes, Fayyad joined her. He asked her how it was going? She said it was awful, all depending on what the Chief had to say. So let's talk about anything else.

Nova told him where Alison had been. Fayyad was appalled at the risk Nova had allowed Alison to take, and reprimanded her for allowing Alison to go there.

She said nothing while he dressed her down. Suppose Alison had been harmed, he said. Killed even?

But Alison had got the info, and was alive, if shaken, she thought, but didn't say. It was Nova's day for reprimands. Don't do this, don't do that. She felt like a five year old on the naughty step.

'What shall we do about the names?' she said, to take the heat off herself.

Fayyad looked them over. Mostly, she got on well with her superior, but he could be a puritan when it came to clothing or the dreaded rule book. His reprimands were short though, and she was practised in distraction. However they got them, they had names.

'I hesitate to say good work,' he said, contemplating the names.

'I couldn't go,' she said. 'And someone had to.'

He raised his hands to stop her saying more. 'A gun, probably the murder weapon. Let's stick with that. I don't want to add to your troubles. But I just wish, Nova...' He stopped, shook his head. 'I don't know what I wish. So, the gun.'

Over the next quarter of an hour, they worked out a strategy, what to do about the illegal gun.

They were crossing the Ts and dotting I's when the assessor returned. Fayyad excused himself and left them.

At least, she'd kept busy and not stewed in uncertainty while the assessor had been upstairs. But nervousness returned, with her future in the balance. Bird gave no clues in his face or stance which way things were going.

He sat down.

'I've had a good chat with Detective Superintendent Martin,' he said. 'And heard the recording you made. She says DI Hawley disputes its veracity.'

'How could I fake such a recording, sir?' exclaimed Nova. 'Where would I get an actress who sounds like Mrs Litt, write her a script, rehearse her...'

Bird put a hand up to stop her tirade.

'Somewhat tricky, I accept. Your Chief believes it is a true recording, and I am willing to go along with that. So my recommendation to the Panel is that the charge against you is dropped.'

Nova gasped. 'You don't know how relieved I am, sir.'

'I can only recommend to the Panel,' he said, holding up a stern hand, 'but with the Chief on your side, it is likely to be accepted.'

'Thank you so much, sir.' She could have got down and kissed his coat tails.

Bird rose and tidied his papers. He put out a hand which she gratefully shook.

'My advice is,' he said, 'whatever you are planning, DC Taylor, don't go and see Jack Bell.'

'What should I do?'

He laughed ruefully. 'This is a new one for me, DC Taylor. A detective assisting a lover charged with murder. Not a textbook case. Please take care. Rules are made for good reasons.'

Chapter 38

Bic was working on the jigsaw which went from bunks to cell wall and necessitated stepping over it with care. He had already completed it twice, each time shaking up the pieces in the box so he could start again with a new mix. He was annoyed there were three pieces missing, blaming Jack for bringing a box without all the pieces. Abandoned, somewhere in Forest Gate nick, Jack told him. 'You don't have to do it.'

Bic ignored this, and upped the ante. He turned the pieces over, so each was blank, and began doing the jigsaw with no pictorial help. No sky, no river, no wagon and horses, just blank card.

It seemed pointless to Jack. But then he reflected jigsaws were, no matter how you did them. Just a way of passing time. Being in clink made him more aware of the necessity, one way or another. Like TV or reading. What wasn't pointless when it came to the crux?

He turned to the book Alison had given him, wondering after a few pages whether aliens did jigsaw puzzles. Is that a sign of intelligence or of having too much time on their hands? Every so often, he looked over at his fellow inmate's obsessive concentration. Down on all fours on the floor, trying piece with piece relentlessly, as if his life depended on it.

Is this how you deal with a seven-year stretch?

As Bic continued, his archipelagoes of pieces stretched across the floor, taking up all the space. Bic was getting increasingly angry, annoyed at everything that was thwarting him. He hated Jack watching him, saying at one point, 'Do you think you're a social worker? Get back to your snotty book and stop staring me out.' His fervency made it difficult for Jack, the cell filled with his companion's frustration.

At one point, Bic threw a handful of pieces against the wall, as if they were conspiring against him. As if somehow they were changing shape when he wasn't looking.

They were going to have a row, Jack was sure of it. Bic had taken over the space. It would be a fight for territory. Jack was already confined to his bunk. He had to confront him.

But how would that work out?

It was so petty. But he must be able to move, breathe, look, without causing a tantrum in his inmate. He wouldn't be pushed into a corner. And maybe, even that wouldn't be enough for this obsessive. Now so incensed, that Jack wondered how to confront him.

He wished he'd never brought in the jigsaw puzzle.

The man was a repeat rapist. Was his compulsion somehow coming out in his treatment of the puzzle? A brutal unreason, with no pleasure in it.

A warden entered.

'You've got a visitor,' he said to Jack.

Jack was instantly relieved to get out of this box. Bic scowled at the warden, who was stepping on the pieces that were widely scattered over the floor.

'Who?'

'Dunno, mate. I'm just the messenger. Let's go.'

Jack had to step on pieces as he left.

'You useless turd!' screamed Bic.

As they walked along the corridor, Jack said to the warden, 'How did I get lumbered with him?'

The warden smiled wryly. 'Difficult, isn't he?'

Jack picked up a hint of intentionality.

'Why me?'

They passed two cells in a row playing the EastEnders theme.

'You hit an inspector,' said the warden.

Was that going to follow him forever? Even here, in Pentonville. It must be on his record. Exaggerated, that failed punch, as if he'd gone around beating up cops by the billion. So he was doomed to suffer continual vengeance, like a damned soul in Hell.

He shook himself. Self pity buttered no parsnips, as his mentor at Alcohol Halt confusingly said.

Why parsnips?

The warden led Jack along several corridors. As they walked, he caught snatches of music behind cell doors and TV vocals. There was a smell of urine mingled with disinfectant, the one battling with the other, neither giving up in the muggy air. This was a zoo of dangerous animals which needed continual mucking out.

How on earth was he going to deal with Bic?

The visitors' room was busy. Prisoners sat at small tables, chairs and tables attached to the floor. To fix the separation distance, he reckoned, and to stop them being used as weapons. All calculated.

The visitors were predominantly women, with a scattering of men, presumably family and friends.

No children, there were other options for family days, Jack had learnt.

Mia, sitting at a far table, half rose and gave him a wave over the heads of visitors and inmates. He crossed to her.

'How on earth did you get in?' he said, sitting opposite her.

Mia shrugged. 'I just came. 16 is the age, I found on their website. I didn't know what to do or where to go, but I saw a group of women at the gate and I asked if they were visiting. They said they were and I just followed. When I got to the visiting area, they told me I wasn't on the list. I should have booked. I told them, I wouldn't do it again but I'd taken time off work specially, and in the end they felt sorry for me. And as you were on remand... They gave me the phone number for next time.'

'It's not easy getting into this place,' said Jack. 'I filled out a mill of papers.'

Mia, not to be outdone, said, 'I got searched, sniffed up and down by a dog.' She threw her hands up. 'What a palaver!'

'It's great to see you. It's a crazy scene here. I've got this awful cellmate. I thought he was OK at first, but now he's totally getting on my nerves.'

'What's he in for?'

He thought of lying, but what was the point? She was old enough.

'He's a rapist.'

'That's rough,' she said, nauseated.

'No choice in the matter,' said Jack. 'We just got thrown in together.' He didn't want to get into a discussion of how it had been fixed. 'He likes jigsaws. More than likes them. He's obsessed with them. He keeps doing that one of yours, The Haywain.'

'Let him keep it, I don't want a jigsaw that's been handled by a rapist.'

'He's doing my head in. We are going to have a fight, I'm sure. I thought, if I keep calm, stick to safe topics, but he won't meet me halfway. It's his sixth time inside, he tells me. Each time he's let out, he goes for a few weeks then does a rape, and keeps going till he's caught.'

'He should be in for life!' exclaimed Mia. 'They should castrate him.'

'I get on with most people, but this guy is off the scale.'

'Better if he'd never been born.'

A ruckus stopped the room. A man in the loose prison gear was yelling at a woman, calling her a useless whore, a stupid cow, and swearing at full volume. Everyone was watching. The man rose and smacked her round the face, she cowering in her seat. Four wardens raced in. They dragged him out struggling and swearing, pointing her out to everyone as useless, as sleeping with the street.

Jack wondered at her life when she'd been living with the man, with no one to halt his violence. Mia had gone pale, thinking similar thoughts no doubt.

This jail was packed with such people. A concentration of violence. The worst thing about being locked up, he was learning quickly, was the other prisoners.

The man gone, the woman had broken down in tears. Another woman came to her, put her arm round her and told her, it wasn't her fault, he was a brute, she was better without him. A little later, the woman was led out of the room, without coercion, the wardens obviously sympathetic.

It took time for the silence to break, everyone comparing their own situation.

'That's the last visit he'll get,' said Jack.

'Who'd want to come,' said Mia, recovering from the outburst. 'That poor woman, what she's had to put up with. And yet, she comes to visit.'

Conversation had begun again, but more subdued. There were tensions in the room, needs and resentments from prisoners and visitors, but these were being played out at a lower tone.

'Did you know,' said Mia, 'that it costs £45 thou a year to keep someone in prison.'

'You are joking,' he said, even as he thought of all the wardens, the form-filling, the office staff, drivers, dog handlers. Food to be supplied, clothing and laundry, teachers, psychologists, the hospital wing.

'I had a KitKat for you,' she said. 'But they wouldn't allow it. No food or drink.'

'It's the thought that counts,' he said, so appreciating the visit of his daughter, and getting out of the enclosure with Bic. 'You don't know how happy I am to see you. A friendly face. Can you keep coming for the next 30 years?'

'Don't you dare say that,' exclaimed Mia. 'Nova and Mum are working their socks off for you. Mum went to find out about the gun. Saw this gangster, schoolmate of yours, Ethan something...'

'Ethan Allen. Yeh. I did some work at his house a few years ago. He's into some dodgy stuff, big time. Fine with me, but don't cross him. What did she find out?'

'She got some names. Nova is investigating them. And oh yes, Mrs Litt has been arrested. Don't think we've just been sitting on our backsides while you've been having it cushy in Pentonville. I was with her when she got arrested, she was going to do a runner...'

There was so much in that bundle. Guns, Mrs Litt arrested, Alison going to a gangster's den.

Things were happening. Somewhat chaotically, but happening.

'I feel so useless in here,' he said.

'Don't think that,' said Mia. 'It's not your fault that the law is dumb. But we are going to get you out, Dad. You've got enough to do, surviving in this dump.'

His eyes welled at the words of his champion.

Chapter 39

Nova was at Tahir's office suite. He was now in sole charge of the empire, and she waved to him as she passed his glass enclosure. He was not her first port of call. She went into the office that had been Tom Litt's, now occupied solely by Sarah Raban. The PA had taken her former boss and lover's desk, her perfume filling the room, the odour seeming to have the purple colour of her lipstick.

No longer the minion, she occupied the space with her boss dead. Her handbag and coat were on the sofa, her own small desk had two bottles of pop and her lunch.

Nova said affably, 'Got a new job yet?'

Raban smiled sweetly. 'Yes, I have. I got an excellent reference. I am starting in a couple of weeks, but I have to tidy up here before I leave.'

Nova might have said something about the increased disorder of her things in the office, but that was not why she was here.

'Get a pay off?' she asked.

'What for?'

Nova smiled at her. She was impressed with Raban's immaculate curly hair. It must cost a fortune keeping it that way. Her boss used to pay for it, now she was responsible for its upkeep.

She hadn't sat down, but was strolling about the office. She looked out of the window at the Olympic Park. There was the swimming pool, the London Stadium, and the spiral sculpture by someone she couldn't remember.

'Nice view,' she said, turning back to the room. 'Now tell me about the gun.'

'What gun?'

But Nova had caught the hint of surprise, the jerk of discomfort. She walked across the room and leaned her straightened arms on the desk, staring fixedly at the PA.

'You have two choices, Ms Raban. One, you can tell me calmly and truthfully about the gun. Or two, I arrest you for misleading a crime investigation.' She paused, watching her quarry. 'You got a pay off, didn't you?'

'Yes,' said Raban weakly.

'How much?'

She maintained her position against the desk, hedging Raban in.

'Five thousand,' she said.

Nova sucked in a breath. 'Not bad, not bad at all, for keeping your mouth shut.' She banged a fist on the desk. 'How many years in prison is it worth?'

Raban shuddered.

'Your boss was murdered,' went on Nova, 'and you kept back evidence about a gun. Can you deny that, Ms Raban?'

The PA was breathing rapidly, looking about her for help, which had no way of getting to her.

'Is not saying something misleading?' she said weakly.

'It most surely is. So let's attempt to put things right. Where did you see the gun?'

She hesitated for a couple of seconds and then pointed to the wall opposite.

'In that safe, there.'

A small safe with a combination was built into the wall.

'Who had access to it?' said Nova.

'Me, my boss Tom and his partner, Tahir.'

'Not Tahir's PA?'

She shook her head. 'He didn't trust her. He's sacked her.'

Nova laughed. This was a swamp of distrust.

'What sort of gun was it?' When Raban hesitated, she added fiercely, 'Come on, come on. You've told me there was a gun. Now give me the details. What sort was it?'

'A pistol.' She covered her face in her hands for a few seconds, then withdrew them with the inevitability of having to come clean. 'It was a shock to see it, on top of papers and the petty cash box. I took it out and looked at it. It was surprisingly heavy.'

'Give me the name, Ms Raban.'

'It had it on the handle. Reminded me of pasta. Penna. I've never heard of a Penna before. It was there a couple of days last week. And then it was gone.' She wiped her eyes with a tissue. 'What will happen to me?'

Nova shrugged. 'It's not in my hands. But it's as well you are providing answers. I advise you, if you know anything that might affect the case, don't hide it. But so far, so good. You will need to come to the station and make a full statement.'

'What about the money I've been given?'

'That's not my concern, Ms Raban. Nor should it be yours. You have been assisting a murderer. That should be your concern, first and foremost.'

'I didn't know. Honest, I didn't.'

Nova laughed. 'Really? Your boss shot dead, and a gun in your safe a few days before. And you didn't know. I'm surprised you were able to get another job. You can't be much of a PA.'

Sarah Raban was pale and shivering. Nova had what she wanted from her. For the moment.

She said, 'I'm wired,' tapping her jacket to indicate the microphone. 'This conversation has been recorded, and my colleague has been listening in. He's in the car park. I shall go down and check in. In about half an hour, I'd like you to come into Tahir's office, with Mr Litt's office diary. And no more shielding. It's going to all come out. So, 30 minutes or so, Sarah. Be ready. You'll see us go into his office. Give us a minute for introductions, then enter on cue.'

Chapter 40

Jack returned to the cell after Mia's visit. He was dreading what he'd find, knowing he'd have to confront Bic who had taken over all the floor space, and emotionally the whole cell. At least, he'd got out of its confines for an hour.

Bic had been foisted on him. Must be Hawley, she would have contacts here, and the order was – make Jack's life miserable. Not beat him up in the shower, though was that to come? Start with putting an obsessive rapist in with him.

The warden opened up the cell. The jigsaw pieces lay all over the floor, as if left behind by a flood that had poured through the cell and drained away. But Bic was in a corner, rocking back and forth, wailing, his knees pulled up to his chest.

'I can't do it, I can't do it,' he moaned, his face constricted in pain.

'Is he always like this?' said Jack to the warden.

'He has a range,' said the warden, 'though somewhat limited,' and closed the cell door.

The wail went on and on.

'I can't do it, I can't do it.'

It struck Jack that this was the tantrum of a four year old. There was not a thing he could do about the obvious cause. Bic was referring to the jigsaw, the pieces turned upside down, and his inability to get anywhere with it. There were six pieces in the middle, supposedly fitting into each other but they looked forced. Jack turned them over; and yes, the pictures on each didn't match up.

Jack looked at the distressed inmate, and half recognised what he was seeing. He had an infant to deal with, as if on a long journey in a car with a child of four with limited attention span, thwarted and bored.

Distraction was the order of the day.

Jack gathered all the jigsaw pieces together. There was no objection from the wailing man, who had been unable to do anything with them. Once together in a mass, he turned the pieces over, showing bits of sky, clouds, river, the wagon. He began to do the jigsaw himself, ignoring Bic. Though it was impossible in the small cell to ignore the rocking, wailing man.

Shut the hell up, he endeavoured not to say, nor give in to an impulse to kick the wailing rapist.

Do the jigsaw.

Jack got all the sky and cloud pieces together. And from these, he sorted out the edge pieces. He didn't like jigsaws that much, lacking the patience for them, but he would pretend complete absorption to shut out the wail, like a Zen monk ignoring thunder and lightning on a mountain top. Not exactly him, he was close to bursting with resentment at having to play-act for this infantile cell mate.

Jack had done the top edge and was working down a side, when Bic crawled over.

'You do the sky,' said Jack hopefully. 'I'll do the river.'

The authoritative parent.

Bic stared at the pieces for a while, as if afraid of them. Then, tentatively, found a piece that fitted. Jack praised him. That was the way, with infants and dogs, praise the action you want. So basic. A pity he didn't have a bag of sweets.

They'd done half the jigsaw, by the time they were let out to go to the server for lunch. Bic didn't want to go, as now the jigsaw was his security blanket, something he could do. Jack with the warden's assistance persuaded him to go for his lunch.

They brought their laden trays back to the cell.

'Eat first,' he said. The parent. Not a job he'd applied for, but if he could control Bic, life in the cell would at least be liveable. Like an unwilling lion tamer who must control the beast or be eaten.

Jack sat on the edge of his bunk, the tray on his knee, Bic on the chair gobbling his lunch, shovelling in the mashed potato and minced meat as if it was a race. Jack had to turn away and concentrate on his own meal, as his fellow inmate's table manners revolted him. The food was barely warm, edible, if a little tasteless. A yogurt to finish with. It filled a hole, though this wasn't the fare for his diabetes that he and a warden had filled in a form for, but he could only deal with one problem at a time.

Before Jack was halfway through his meal, Bic was back at the jigsaw. He joined him once he had finished. And it wasn't so bad. Bic had calmed down now he was being creative. He hated being thwarted; Jack would have to watch for that. A depressing thought, he could be stuck with Bic for months.

Back to the river pieces and the wagon and horses drinking. Don't think ahead. But you couldn't tell yourself not to think something. Ahead was where he was going. This place, this inmate, his trial.

They completed the jigsaw in about an hour. Bic wanted to mix up the pieces and start again. But Jack said no. He wanted to burn the jigsaw, throw it in a canal. He couldn't bear to do it ever again.

With his notebook and a couple of pens, they played noughts and crosses. A simple game that Jack knew backwards through playing with Mia when she was about six. Between the two of them, father and daughter, they had worked out the strategy. If you went first and didn't make a mistake, you couldn't lose. Except Jack wasn't playing to win, most of the time. He was giving three quarters of the games to Bic.

Jack suggested they play hangman, but that had to be given up when it was obvious that Bic was barely literate. So they played battleships and cruisers, drawing a grid of twenty by twenty and putting in the pieces of the fleet in the various squares. The grid squares were numbered down the side, and lettered across the top. And then in turns, you called out a square, such as B16, in which each would put a big cross. A miss, the other would say most likely, or occasionally, Hit.

Pure luck who destroyed whose fleet first. Except Jack cheated to make sure Bic won.

Then paper aeroplanes. Why was he doing all this? For a rapist, with the emotional responses of a six year old. For some peace, some space. Like an exhausted parent with an overactive child, wondering if he would ever grow up.

They flew their planes, the winner went the furthest. It got more sophisticated with three planes each. He gave his best flyer to Bic, dying to get back to his book, but knew he had to control Bic if he was to get time to himself. He was the adult here. Later, if he could, he'd phone Mia and ask her to bring in a pack of playing cards. More paper, as his notebook was all used up. Some of her children's games: Ludo, Snakes & Ladders, Happy Families.

He was depressed at planning such a future. But Bic was happy. Jack just wished that Bic's mother would come and take him home.

Chapter 41

Nova and Fayyad entered Tahir's glass walled office.

He was at his desk, his jacket on a hanger behind him, sleeves rolled up, the air-conditioning blowing a cooling breeze. Tahir obviously liked it chilly. At the police station, the air conditioning was off, as the Chief said Net Zero was their target. No more bottled water, it was tap water or nothing, and air con only when it was unbearable.

'What's this in honour of?' said Tahir with a nervous smile.

'This is my boss, Detective Inspector Kamani.'

'How do you do?' said Tahir, noting with alarm that two uniformed officers had just arrived outside his office.

Fayyad said, 'You are in sole charge here now?' strolling about the office and looking out the window at the Olympic Park.

'Yes, I am. With the sad death of my partner, Tom.'

He was breathing rapidly. Two cops in his room, two uniformed officers outside. Too many for a social call. Something was up.

Sarah Raban entered holding a large desk diary which she held up for Nova's benefit.

Why such a short skirt? thought Nova, more aware of it with the attention of the male coppers. Was that all she had in her wardrobe?

Her boss was trying hard not to look at Raban's shapely, tanned legs. Which perhaps had got Sarah her new job, men being men.

'Tell us about the gun,' said Fayyad.

Tahir looked about him nervously. 'Do I need a solicitor?'

'I don't know,' said Fayyad. 'Do you?'

'The gun,' reminded Nova. 'You were about to tell us about the gun?'

Tahir waved his hands in negation. 'I don't know anything about a gun.'

'We have information that you bought it,' said Nova. Which was true, but they would not get a statement from Ethan Allen, the pretend estate agent. That had been the deal.

'Information from who?' he demanded.

'We are asking the questions,' said Fayyad. 'The gun, concentrate on the gun.'

'Where did you say it was, Ms Raban?' said Nova, turning to the PA, revealing she had been spilling the beans.

Raban froze like a hare in a car's headlights. She swallowed, finding it difficult to speak. She had said things in one room which she hadn't wanted brought in here.

Never trust a cop.

'In the safe,' she managed to say, not daring to look at Tahir who was glaring at her.

'You were given a payoff,' said Nova. 'How much?'

Raban hesitated, looking about her for help which wasn't going to come. She avoided Tahir's evil eye which was fast losing its power.

'Five thousand pounds,' she said.

She had closed her eyes, standing helpless, clutching the office diary as if it was a teddy.

'Just right for a world cruise, with plenty of spending money,' said Nova. 'So much. What was it for?'

Raban looked about helplessly, rocking as if about to fall.

Fayyad rushed in with a chair.

'Please sit down, Ms Raban.'

Raban sank onto the seat. 'Thank you.'

'You were about to tell us why you got the pay off?'

'For redundancy,' interrupted Tahir. 'Wasn't that so, Miss Raban?'

Fayyad said, 'Please let her answer of her own accord. Why did you get the payoff, Ms Raban?'

She shook her head, 'I am sorry, Mr Ahmed, but I can't spend money in jail. I have to look after myself.' She turned to Nova, then Fayyad, unsure who she should answer to. 'Mr Ahmed gave me the money to forget about the gun.'

'A lie! A dirty lie!' declared Tahir. 'It was redundancy money to Tom Litt's whore.'

'Please don't call me names, Mr Ahmed. You will regret it. I know too much. You told me to forget ever seeing the gun. You paid me five thousand for that. Do you want it back?'

Tahir didn't reply.

She turned to Fayyad, 'The safe is in my office. I see the comings and goings. Mr Ahmed tried to sneak the gun out of the safe, but I saw him doing it.'

'More lies!' he screamed. 'How can you trust a woman like that!'

'When was that?' said Nova, ignoring Tahir's outburst.

'Monday morning, 9 am,' said Raban. She opened up the desk diary which was covering her knees, as if suddenly aware of the shortness of her skirt.

DI Hawley came into the office.

'What on earth is going on here?' she said, looking around at Fayyad, Nova, Tahir and the PA.

'We are investigating a murder,' said Fayyad.

'What murder?'

'The murder of Tom Litt,' he said.

'We have the murderer in jail!' exclaimed Hawley. 'Jack Bell.'

'Jack Bell is in jail, ma'am,' said Nova. 'That's true. But he isn't the murderer.'

Hawley pushed her backwards on both shoulders. 'You are on a charge of gross misconduct, DC Taylor. How dare you interfere with my case!'

Nova felt no desire to tell her the charge was most likely cancelled. Nor that Hawley's visit here had been prearranged with the Chief. She could take being pushed about; anger made people less restrained.

Hawley turned on Fayyad.

'How dare you interfere with my witnesses! You and your pipsqueak assistant have been attempting to foul up my investigation from the start. I will not have it. I intend reporting this as soon as I am back at the station.'

She eyed them, hands on hips. She would show them who was the boss. She had priority. Rules were rules.

'We have the Chief's permission,' said Fayyad.

'I don't believe you.'

'Phone her. Or just speak up. She's in her office, listening in on us,' said Fayyad. He held up his phone.

She eyed him quizzically. 'I don't get this. What's going on, Kamani?

'It is becoming more and more apparent that you have charged the wrong person.'

'The blood in his van!' yelled Hawley. 'The affair he was having with Mrs Litt!'

'No, he wasn't,' intervened Nova. 'You were having an affair with her. You! We have Mrs Litt's phone and her texts to you. The two of you were lovers.'

'Shut your subordinate up,' screamed Hawley. 'She is a serial liar to protect her killer builder!'

'You were having an affair with Mrs Litt,' repeated Nova. 'You got her to scrub out the bedroom so there'd be no evidence you were ever there. As you were, for very many days and weeks.'

'Lies on lies!' She looked wildly about her, then stiffened, taking a deep breath, as she reasserted herself. 'I am the investigating officer here, and I am arresting this junior for interfering in the course of justice.'

Nova was about to protest, but Fayyad put his finger to his lips, a signal to let him take matters forward.

'You can make your case shortly, DI Hawley,' he said. 'I'm sure it will be most informative, and you may change your mind. But let's listen to Ms Raban. She has important information, I am sure you will want to hear.' He turned to the PA. 'You were saying that at 9am on Monday, Mr Ahmed took the gun out of the safe. Where was he going with it?'

Raban referred to the desk diary on her knees. She had been a silent witness to Hawley's tirade, rapidly working out what she must do to stay out of jail.

'Mr Litt and Mr Ahmed had an appointment at 9.15 am at 32 Windsor Road,' she said. 'They left together. That's all I can tell you, sir. I didn't know who they were meeting or what it was about. Believe me.'

Fayyad turned to Tahir. 'You had the gun when you left here with Tom Litt. Did you kill him?'

'No.' He was playing with a shirt sleeve, unravelling it, then ravelling it. 'She did.' He indicated Hawley. 'I'm not taking the rap for murder. We met her at Windsor Road.' He pointed her out, as if in the witness box, as well he might be. 'I gave her the gun.' He looked at Fayyad and Nova, his hands shaking, a plea in his eyes. 'She said I had to bring it to her or she'd have me for being in possession of an illegal weapon.'

'Another liar in a nest of liars!' yelled Hawley. 'What a dirty, put up case, DI Kamani!'

She looked around wildly, turned and burst out of the office door. Fayyad raced after her.

'Hold her!' he yelled to the two uniformed officers.

They wouldn't let her pass, having been pre-warned that DI Hawley was going to be arrested.

'Let me through!' she exclaimed. 'This is an illegal arrest!'

She tried to pull away from them, but the two officers held her as Fayyad snapped on the handcuffs.

Chapter 42

Fayyad and Nova were seated in the Chief's office.

'You two are filling up the cells in the station,' she said with a wry smile.

Nova could feel a weariness in the Chief. Getting Hawley was one thing but it had implications for the Chief's future.

'Can we get Jack released, ma'am?' said Nova.

The Chief shrugged. 'Much as I'd like to, I can't do it, DC Taylor. That's down to the Crown Prosecution Service. Jack Bell has been sent by the magistrate's court to the crown court for trial. The CPO have said there's a strong case against him. They are loath to admit being mistaken, as I well know. They will want to see all the evidence we have, all the statements. They are slow to catch up.'

Tell me something new, thought Nova.

'So how is the interviewing going?' said the Chief.

'Mrs Litt is at last talking,' said Fayyad. 'When we told her DI Hawley had been arrested, she gave up on her no comments. She admits she and Hawley were lovers. Hawley decided to get rid of her husband, and seeing Jack was working there, it was convenient to throw the blame on him.'

'With herself as investigating officer,' added Nova, 'making it all the easier. She made sure no other avenues were looked at.'

'How did Tahir Ahmed come into it?' said the Chief.

'Mrs Litt knew that her husband and Ahmed were quarrelling, so they drew him in. He had to obtain the gun and get Litt to the rendezvous where Hawley was waiting. Ahmed gave her the gun when he arrived. We think he was there for the shooting, as Hawley would have needed a hand getting the body into the boot of her car. Then Ahmed sped off to Worthing, his alibi.'

'And the blood in Jack's van?'

'He keeps it open a lot of the time when he is working, ma'am,' said Nova, 'so it would have been easy enough to scatter some blood inside.'

'And the shenanigans on Wanstead Flats? Who was involved?'

'We think Hawley and Ahmed drove there with the body,' said Fayyad. 'They knew Jack was there as they had a GPS tracker attached to his van, and he'd told Mrs Litt earlier he'd be out with his telescope on the Flats. Hawley and Ahmed dumped the body, Ahmed cried out: help me, help me, to draw Jack in. And the two of them drove off before he could identify them.'

'Jack was suckered in,' said Nova. 'He finds the body of his client, very puzzled how it got there, and phones the ambulance service and police. Fifteen minutes later, back comes DI Hawley, ready to pour it all on Jack.'

'Three of them in it,' said the Chief. 'Are we clear on their motives?'

'Mrs Litt gets rid of her bully of a husband, she gets his money, a share of the firm, and the house,' said Nova. 'Ahmed gets control of the firm. DI Hawley has her lover to herself, now rich, and has a result to impress you with.'

'A little impertinent, DC Taylor, but it's deserved.' She shook her head in admission of her own fault. 'As soon as this case is wrapped up, we are going to have to look back at DI Hawley's prior cases. That will be a can of worms, as I suspect this won't be the only case she has fixed.'

'The sooner we can get on with that the better, ma'am,' said Fayyad. 'It could be a major scandal.'

'I have no doubt,' said the Chief. 'The media will love it. So we need to get into Hawley's back cases as a priority, before it all blows up on us.'

Nova was well aware that the Chief was in line for the blame if Hawley had been fixing cases. Fayyad had said if it's really bad, she may be forced to retire. Not a good way to end a career.

A great pity, thought Nova. She liked the Chief, she was fair, she listened. But she was also Hawley's immediate boss, and too accepting of her successes. So if Hawley had a line of frame-ups, the Chief was number one for the chop.

Chapter 43

Mia was sitting on a low wall, outside a block of luxury apartments on the Isle of Dogs. She shivered. It was raining lightly, and she wished she was wearing a coat, but it had been fine when she'd left home. It had started to rain when she was on the bus.

The apartments had large balconies overlooking the river, she could see furniture on them and tumbling plants. You had to be well off to live here.

Last night, Alison, Nova and herself had talked over where things were. Hawley arrested, Mrs Litt talking non-stop. And Jack still in clink. The whole case had unravelled, yet he was still in clink.

Mia had a plan of sorts, half a plan you might say. She couldn't let Nova and her mother get all the glory. She looked again at the business card. Mary Marat, Solicitor. She had met her on a demo. They had held a large banner between them: Keep the oil in the soil! Keep the coal in the hole! Mary was utterly into eco causes, and seemed to know everyone. Well connected, as they say. Later that day, Mia had phoned her from a police station. 'Get me out of here!'

And Mary had worked her magic.

Mia had her number in her contacts. Of course, she might not be in, though she said she often worked from home. Today? She rubbed her arms, she wanted to get out of the rain. Be in. Her plan, as vague as it was, began with her just turning up. She could explain herself better in person.

She took a deep breath. Begin.

Mia phoned. And waited, listening to the pulse in those indeterminate seconds.

'Hello. Mary Marat.'

At least, she was at the end of her phone.

'I'm Mia Bell. If you remember, you got me out of jail about six months ago...'

'Oh yes. The young lady with all the hair... We shared a banner. Are you on a demo? In trouble?'

'It's complicated,' she said. 'Are you at home?'

'I am.'

'Well, I'm just outside.'

'And getting wet. You'd best come up, Mia. I need a break from these contracts. We'll have a cup of tea, and you can tell me what you've been up to.'

The call ended. That wasn't so difficult, she thought. Now to find out just how well connected Mary Marat is. Who she knew, where. To get Jack out of Pentonville.

Mia crossed the quiet street, glanced at the business card for the apartment number, and pressed the button. Mia was answered almost at once. She replied, identities agreed, she was buzzed in.

Chapter 44

Jack couldn't sleep, Bic above him was snoring like a pair of mating hippos. He had tried earplugs, shoving his head under the pillow, both next to useless. He shook Bic awake, who mumbled, 'Sorry, mate,' stayed quiet for five minutes and then returned to his blasts. Throughout the night, Jack shook him a few more times to get the same, 'Sorry, mate,' and a quick return to the stentorian notes.

He hadn't appreciated his spell in Forest Gate nick. There, he'd had a cell to himself. Here, he had a rapist, half child, who needed continual stimulation, and thanked him by snoring throughout the night.

In the morning, he felt wretched. He told Bic, he'd snored all night.

'Everyone does,' said Bic with a shrug. 'It's just a question of who gets to sleep first.'

There was Bic's questionable morality. Everyone does it. So jump the gun.

After breakfast, Bic was taken away for an induction course. He'd done them before, he said, but it got him out of the cell and he could meet the newcomers and be the voice of experience. Jack was more than happy to see him go. As a prisoner on remand, he was excluded from induction courses. He couldn't see the logic of it, as he was going to be here some time and needed to understand how things worked, what he could do or get, and when.

Like a TV set. He heard them as he passed cells. What were the rules on getting one? But there was another priority. Could he get a transfer to another cell? With a less demanding, quieter, fellow inmate.

He stretched out on his bunk and slept, a troubled sleep, with a chorus of battleships and cruisers, jigsaws and aeroplanes, and a chisel-faced jury who all agreed he had a guilty look. His eyes too close together, his curly hair, his cracked thumbnail, all added proof, if more proof were ever needed, they decided.

He was shaken awake by a warden.

'You've got a visitor, mate.'

Jack arose, sleep in his eyes. He rapidly sluiced his face, and followed the warden along the corridor.

'How do I get a transfer to another cell?' he said. 'This guy is driving me crackers.'

'I'll get you a form,' said the warden.

A depressing answer. First he had to get the form, then fill it in, then get it taken to whoever assessed forms, with his, no doubt, at the bottom of a tower of forms. It would eventually get to the top by the time Jack had died through lack of sleep. Or he had killed Bic. If he was going to go down for murder, he might as well kill the obvious candidate.

He was surprised to see Nova in the visitors' room. There was no one else there, as this wasn't a regular visiting hour.

Pleased to see her, he said, 'I thought you were warned off seeing me.'

'Things have changed,' she said. And filled him in on what Alison and Mia had been up to, on Hawley's arrest, Mrs Litt singing like a turtle dove, and Tahir loading everything on Hawley. While Hawley's interview consisted of no comment to every question. Revealing in itself. Her house was being searched this very minute.

'You are in the clear,' she said, after her lengthy explanation.

This took some processing. Alison, Nova and Mia had been busy. The main players, with Fayyad assisting, while he had been in another world, one the size of a cell. Mia had said they were working to get him off. He'd taken it like the white lies to a dying relative. Well meant but untrue.

And now Nova was saying they had done it. There had to be a hole in it.

'You say I'm in the clear. So when do I get out?'

She shrugged. 'Wish I knew, love. But the statements from Mrs Litt and Tahir Ahmed have to go to the CPS, along with all the new evidence. They will read every word 20 times over. They'll get your file out, go through that over and over with a red pen.'

'While I grow old and grey.'

'The Chief is trying to hurry them up, but they have only one gear. Dead slow. But you are innocent, my love. It is proven.'

She squeezed his hand across the table. The best they could do in intimacy.

'I should be over the moon, but I am so exhausted. I have the most awful cell mate,' he said. 'During the day I have to keep him entertained, and he thanks me by snoring like a tribe of pigs all night.'

'I am so sorry,' she said.

'I keep thinking, how can I get out of this cell. Beyond strangling him.'

'Don't do anything crazy, please, Jack. You'll be out in a few days, I'm sure.'

'How long is a few? Two days, three, a month?'

She couldn't say. Who knew?

'Sorry to moan,' he said. 'I must just pace it out day by day. At least, I know I'm on the way out, however tortuous that might be. I've got to keep telling myself that this is good news. Of course it is. But a night without sleep makes jail-time endless. Sorry to be so ungrateful. Ultra sorry. I have to see it as it is. There will be no trial, hooray.'

A weak hooray. Tiredness had deadened any enthusiasm.

'Me, Alison or Mia will visit you every day. Just don't do anything dumb.'

'I'm going to get a pack of forms for everything and keep their back office so busy...' he began and stopped as a warden approached.

'The Governor wants to see you both.'

Jack whistled. 'We are going up in the world.'

'It's like seeing the King,' said Nova blowing out her cheeks.

'Only harder,' said the warden. 'Don't know who you two have been paying off.'

They followed him along various corridors, up stairs, away from the sounds and smells of the prison. Here were busy office workers with computers. Did forms get sent here? There was a lot of paperwork on the desks, he noted. All those forms filled in when he first came: health, food, religion, employment, sexual orientation, what did they do with them all?

Pass them around to keep themselves busy.

The warden took them to a large door labelled Governor's Office. The warden knocked. A woman came to the door.

'Jack Bell and DC Taylor,' said the warden.

The woman went inside, and returned a few moments later. From which Jack gathered that the woman was the secretary.

'Come in,' she said.

Nova and Jack entered, the warden staying outside.

The Governor sat at a large desk in a dark, wood-lined room with a large portrait of the King behind her, reminding Jack of the magistrate's court. The room was spacious with book-filled shelves around the walls. There were long, green, paisley drapes at the windows. It was a room of rank.

The Governor came out from behind her desk. She was wearing a navy blue suit with a green tie and pinkish shirt. Nova wondered if she were colour blind, but of course it was not the thing to say.

She was a tall, middle-aged woman, her hair greying, and tied at the top in an efficient bun.

'I am Georgie Smith, Governor of Pentonville Prison,' she said, 'and you are Jack Bell, and DC Taylor.'

'We are, ma'am.'

'How do I get a transfer away from my screwed-up cellmate?' burst out Jack.

If not here, where? Surely, she could trample through the paperwork.

'We'll get to that,' she said with a smile. 'Very soon.'

'My cellmate is a rapist and mentally ill,' he said.

'More than half of our inmates have mental illnesses of one sort or another,' said the Governor with a weary sigh, as if this was beyond her capabilities. 'And I am afraid rape is not a rare crime in Pentonville.' She held up a hand, 'But have patience, Mr Bell.'

She turned to her secretary who was at her desk.

'Amy,' said the Governor, 'could you bring out the TV screen?'

Amy pushed a large TV screen on wheels to where they all could see it.

'This is a recording from earlier this morning,' said the Governor. 'From Breakfast on BBC1. Play it please, Amy.'

This had to be important, Jack was thinking. You don't get to the Governor's office for tittle tattle or to watch chatter on TV. Most prisoners never got here, ever. It must be to do with the case against him collapsing. Wake, pay attention.

He crossed his fingers behind his back.

The video began playing. And there was Mia on a sofa in a TV studio. Jack laughed, her hair was as wild as ever. She hadn't let make-up people touch it.

'My daughter, my daughter...' he managed to say. 'That's Mia. What's she doing on TV?'

Nova put a hand on his shoulder. 'Let's hear her, Jack.'

'My father, Jack Bell, was framed,' said Mia, unstoppably rapid, 'by Detective Inspector Hawley, for the murder of

Tom Litt. Blood was planted in his van, and Mrs Litt claimed she was my father's lover. But it was all a frame-up.'

On Mia rolled, like the express to the Scottish Highlands.

'Mrs Litt has now admitted she was lying. My dad was just at her house to do some bricklaying. She is in Forest Gate Police Station and telling the truth at long last. Detective Inspector Hawley has been arrested for the murder. A copper killer! The case against my dad is in tatters. But he remains in jail.'

'Why do you think that is?' said a woman off camera.

'Because the police don't want to admit how corrupt they are. They protect their own.'

Jack was impressed, she was a natural. Mia leaned forward to speak to the camera. It was as if she was talking to him alone.

'How many others has Hawley framed?', she went on. 'In my dad's case, she arrested an innocent man and fixed all the evidence against him. Now this is out in the open, why is he still in Pentonville?'

She stared into the camera, holding the question for the millions eating toast and drinking coffee.

'I demand a public enquiry into this case, and into all the cases Detective Inspector Hawley has been responsible for. How many innocent people has she sent to prison to further her reputation?'

'This is an evolving story,' said the woman interviewer, as the camera switched onto her on another sofa. 'We will follow it up. Thank you, Mia Bell.'

The shot switched to a man in a busy street with a microphone.

'Have you caught a bus recently?' he said cheerily into camera.

'No,' said Jack. 'But I hope to before I die.'

'Switch off, Amy,' said the Governor.

She did so, before the man could begin telling them about buses, and wheeled the screen away.

Jack had been holding back tears as he listened to his daughter. The wondrous cheek of her. How on earth had she got into a TV studio? But she'd certainly given both barrels. And it had to be, more or less, true or they wouldn't have had her on.

Mia was telling the world that her father had been framed by a crooked cop. Sleeplessness was draining away in the new reality. It must be true. It was on TV!

The world had speeded up, and he was working hard to catch up.

'I saw it live,' said the Governor, 'a couple of hours ago while I was eating my breakfast. There's been quite a fuss over it.'

'Who from?' said Jack, wanting to know who his daughter had annoyed.

She smiled indulgently.

'The Home Office, to begin with. The Minister was watching too. She didn't like the accusation that we are holding an innocent man. That is heavy enough,' said the Governor. 'And then, the added accusation of extensive police corruption.' She shook her head. 'Over breakfast too. I am so glad Pentonville is in the clear. There's dirty business going on in Forest Gate, Mr Bell. But that's by the by. We are here to deal with you. After watching your daughter's accusations, there was a fury of phone calls. First the Minister to me. She somewhat put me on the spot as I wasn't up on your case. I had to put that right immediately. More calls coming in, going out, including one to Chief Superintendent Nikki Martin at Forest Gate. And she said categorically that Jack Bell is innocent, that the case against you was shredded. We both consulted the CPS, who were in a tizzy with the Minister at them non-stop. The media doorstepping her. Oh, fun and games! I haven't enjoyed myself so much in years.'

She laughed raucously, hands on hips, a tear rolling down her face. Jack and Nova looked to each other, this was not the behaviour you expected of a prison governor.

When at last, the Governor had somewhat calmed down, she said:

'Thank your daughter, Mr Bell. You are a free man.'

Jack was stunned. Nova too for an instant, and then embraced him as if he had just won a gold medal for the 100 metres.

'It's over, Jack!'

'I can leave,' he said hesitantly, as if the Governor was play acting, wondering what was the catch.

'You most surely can. The sooner you are off the premises the better. No offence intended, but we are getting phone calls non-stop from the media. I want to say to them: Jack Bell has been released. Now go and harass someone else, please. You are a free man, sir, no longer in the custody of His Majesty. Go to your cell, collect your things, take them to reception where you will be signed out.'

She held out her hand for Jack to shake. He took it.

'I hope your stay in Pentonville wasn't too arduous.'

Chapter 45

Nova waited at reception, while Jack was in his cell throwing the few things he had into a cardboard box. He could have easily left the lot behind. Maybe just take Alison's book.

Free! In utter disbelief. He was a free man, he was dancing as he packed. Get out of here before they change their mind.

Bic returned with a warden.

'What you doing, mate?' he said, seeing Jack packing.

'I'm off,' said Jack.

'What, another clink?'

'No, I'm off out of here. I am free. The evidence against me is phony.' He had no wish to go into details.

Bic flushed with misery.

'It always happens, I get a decent cell mate and they move him on. We had some good times, didn't we, mate?'

When? thought Jack.

'I've had some dregs as cell mates, real scum, but you have been the best.'

Jack looked him over in his baggy clothing, almost bald. In and out of prison for much of his adult life.

'Can I give you some advice?'

'Sure, mate.'

He wondered whether to say it, knew it would do no good.

'Rapists are rats. You can be better than that, Bic.'

Bic took a step towards him and pushed him backwards, scowling. 'Don't you go all social worker on me. You're like all the rest! Filthy scumbag.'

Jack exited the cell with his box.

You can be better. That's what they'd said to him at Alcohol Halt in his alcoholic days, but only if you want to be. There was little sign of that in Bic. He would die in prison.

Jack had left behind the jigsaw. Not as a present, but Mia wouldn't want it back, nor would he ever want to do it again.

Jack was escorted through the hallways, his heart pumping, unbelievable joy, like a child seeing the sea for the first time and racing into the surf.

Reception was slow. Maybe the Governor wanted him out, but bureaucracy wouldn't be stifled so easily. Forms had to be filled in, his mobile phone, keys and credit card to be returned and signed for. Nova was there and had brought him tea and biscuits.

A prison van had drawn up and new inmates were coming in. Which one of those would be thrown in with Bic? Poor guy. He hoped he had earplugs. And a new jigsaw.

They were let out at the front of the prison. One of those cliches, the old lag coming out through the high iron doors. The sky, all that sky. He had missed it, just seen it in a jigsaw, and a strip in the exercise yard.

Jack waited, box in arms, while Nova went to get her vehicle. He watched the buses and the people walking by. He was one of them again.

No shackles, no smell of urine. He did a little jig.

An old woman passing by, with a basket on wheels, looked at him weirdly.

'I'm free!' he told her.

Her expression suggested she wasn't sure he should be.

Well, he was. And would need to think how he was going to live. How much money did he have in the bank? A job that he'd only been half paid for. But he was free and that was worth so much. Free to make his own decisions, to go where he wanted.

To get work. Return to normality.

Jack enjoyed the drive back to Forest Gate. Nova put the radio on a music channel, quietly, as they conversed. She suggested a night out with the telescope in a few days.

'Not on Wanstead Flats,' he said.

'You have to go back there,' she said. 'Otherwise Hawley wins.'

'Only if you come.'

They agreed on that.

A little later, she said to him, 'Do you know about Burke and Hare?'

'Grave robbers in Scotland, weren't they?'

She nodded. 'In the 1820s. They robbed graves for the medical schools of Edinburgh. Till they found they got more money, with a better class of body, if they killed them themselves. The doctors who got the bodies may have suspected, but they didn't look too close.'

He made the connection. 'DI Hawley?'

'She was getting the results. No one looked too closely at how. In fact, she was due to be promoted to Chief Inspector.'

'If what you are saying is true...' thinking of himself and those that fought for his release, 'how many innocent people are doing a long stretch because of her?'

'And what's her body count?'

'You think she killed more than Tom Litt?'

'I wouldn't rule it out.'

That took some processing. What a corrupt detective inspector could do. And how the system backed her up. He'd seen it close up.

Nova dropped him off at home, she had to get back to the station. There was lots to do on the case. Interviews, paperwork, and to catch up with progress while she'd been away.

He went into the flat, and was pleased to find it had been tidied up. The cops had been here with the forensic team, though they couldn't have found anything worthwhile unless it had been planted. All the dishes had been washed

191

up in the kitchen. Not the forensic guys. Must be the house fairies. There was even food in the fridge. Bless those fairies.

Jack had a long shower to wash away the odour of prison. He washed his hair, he shaved and then went to bed. The house fairies had even ventured into the bedroom and put on clean sheets.

Chapter 46

That evening, Alison invited him over for a meal. It was a warmish, spring evening, when he strolled over, light was leaving the sky, the clouds purple, an orange furnace streaking the west. That would have been a major penalty of a long sentence, losing the night sky. To be in a concrete box without stars and planets. Without the moon and the constellations.

Jack almost bumped into a tree, as he was walking, looking upwards to identify the first of his old friends. And then the oddity, the trees had leaves. Locked in concrete, he had not seen a single one.

All this space.

He was here alone, walking down the road. So everyday, but in prison, he was either with Bic or accompanied by a warden. The luxury of being in the street by himself, with such a volume of air above and around him, was beyond a King's ransom.

Jack reflected on how long it had taken him to accept they were letting him go. Even outside the jail waiting for Nova, a bit of him expected a gang of wardens to rush out, handcuff him and say: 'We made a mistake, mate. Back you go!'

Nova had told him in the visitors' room that they were dropping the charge. He'd only half believed her as the reality was Pentonville. The keys, the bars and locked door, the noise and violence, the smell of urine and futility. It was only in the Governor's office, the fantasy of being there at all, then Mia on TV, and being told by the man, who was a woman, that he was free.

Not a lie, nor a trick, but an admission that his arrest and charge had been based on lies and faked evidence.

Burke and Hare had got their comeuppance.

Alison opened the door. She was wearing a short sleeved summer dress with a floral pattern. She smiled with joy and embraced him.

'Welcome back, Jack.'

He thanked her, and she led him through the hallway and on to the garden patio. There, to be met by applause and whoops.

There was no great crowd, but all the right people: Alison, Nova, Mia and Fayyad. They embraced him, shook his hand and welcomed him back to the land of the free.

'Speech, speech!' exclaimed Mia, dressed in the same t-shirt and jeans as she had been wearing in the TV studio.

'Let's hear the free man!' called Fayyad.

Jack's eyes welled as he looked at them all on the patio. He was unable to speak for a few seconds; here were those who had got him out.

'I am absolutely grateful for all you have done for me,' he managed to say. 'I was charged with murder. Utterly stitched up by a corrupt cop. If you hadn't uncovered the evidence of a conspiracy, I'd be on my way to a life sentence. Thank you all. You got me out.'

They cheered and clapped. He bathed in the applause, his face reddening. Happy, a little embarrassed. But free.

'Tell me, Mia,' he said, 'how did you get into the BBC?'

She shrugged, as if it was such a little thing. 'I had met this solicitor on a demo who had contacts. So I phoned her. And she gave me the number of a BBC journalist. I phoned, gave her the spiel and said I'd go to ITV if the BBC weren't interested. She said she needed to do some fact checking. Fifteen minutes later, she got back to me. She'd phoned Forest Gate Police Station and they'd confirmed all I'd said. And would I come into the studio.'

'You were magnificent,' said Alison, embracing her. 'A proper star. But I do wish you'd brushed your hair.'

Mia beamed as she was roundly applauded.

'And you, Alison,' said Jack. 'Tell me about tracking down the gun.'

'Oh no,' exclaimed Alison, her hands rushing to her face to hide the horror. 'I shall never forget being locked in the stock room by that gang boss. I am a natural born coward, Jack. Never ever will I go and find a gun for anyone, for anything, for the rest of my life.'

'But you did it, Mum,' said Mia.

'Never again, not ever. My charges are little children, staff meetings, not drug barons and pimps. I am a respectable headteacher and want to stay that way until I retire, not bundled up and tossed in the River Lea.'

Nova embraced her. 'You did a great job.'

'You were sceptical, Fayyad,' said Jack.

Fayyad shook his head. 'Shame on me, Jack, but I didn't realise how corrupt DI Hawley was. She had an open and shut case against you, till Nova got that recording from Mrs Litt, and then I began to realise it was a stitch up.'

'But when you saw it, you gave one hundred per cent support,' said Nova, standing up for her boss. 'Organising the get-together at Tahir's office to ensnare Hawley.'

Fayyad got his round of applause. It was one of those evenings.

As an encore, he added, 'I've got your keys, Jack.' He threw them to Jack who caught them. 'The van's in the station car park with your telescope inside.'

Jack flashed his hands in mock fear. 'I'm not going back there. The food is awful, the company dreadful.'

Nova took the keys from his hand. 'I'll pick up your van, Jack. If you admit we are not all pigs.'

'Not all, I admit,' said Jack. 'Not Fayyad, not you. You got the recording from Mrs Litt, you got Tom Litt's PA talking... '

'And I got myself charged with gross misconduct for visiting you,' she said, somewhat overwhelmed by the praise heaped on her.

She fussed with the scrunchie around her ponytail.

'No more kind words,' she said. 'I did what I had to.' She took Jack by the arm. 'And now, please excuse us, everyone. I've a few words to say to Jack in private.'

She drew him down the garden path. Mia wolf-whistled as Jack and Nova disappeared into the greenery. The others returned to the food and drink laid out on the table, to gossip and to bonhomie, like a track team that has brought home the cup.

Jack and Nova were in the shrubbery. They sat on a bench, the others not visible, just the patio light through the foliage.

'No wardens, no prison visitors,' said Nova. 'Just me and you for a change.'

'I missed you.'

'We'd had a row,' she said. 'Remember?'

'Yes. You said we should cool off for a month.'

'I don't recall that,' she said. Though she did.

She squeezed his hand. A welcome of welcomes, an evaporation of sins.

'I can't help being busy, Jack,' she said. 'I am a detective. It's the way it is.'

'I get it,' he said, 'but don't ever leave me at the Picturehouse by myself.'

'Sorry. Utterly, sincerely, completely.'

'See what that led to!'

She laughed, guiltily. 'She was going to get you one way or another, Jack.'

He so agreed. 'If not on the Flats,' he said, 'she'd have dumped the body outside my front door.'

'Rang the bell and raced away, like kids playing Knock Down Ginger.'

Bridge Over Troubled Water was playing quietly on the patio. A half moon was rising in the south east.

Nova and Jack embraced in the purple light.

Thank you!

I am grateful to every reader who finishes one of my novels. I have taken you on a journey which I hope you have enjoyed. There are plenty of things you could have been doing, other than reading this book. So, thank you for your time. If you liked *Jack In Clink*, here's what you can do next:

I'd appreciate a review. In that way, you can help me tell other readers about my books. Without reviews authors get few sales. So I'd be grateful for your review to help this series get on the move.

You can get a FREE ebook of *Murder at Any Price* if you sign up for my readers' list.

You may give it to a friend if you wish. When you sign up for my readers' list you will receive my regular newsletter. This will give you news about me, what I'm reading, and tell you about my future books, PLUS a variety of giveaways.

Sign up at my website:
DerekSmithWriter.com

Books by DH Smith

Jack Bell

These are all standalone novels and can be read in any order. They are:

- *Jack of All Trades*
- *Jack of Spades*
- *Jack o'Lantern*
- *Jack By The Hedge*
- *Jack In The Box*
- *Jack On The Tower*
- *Jack Recalled*
- *Jack At Death's Door*
- *Jack At The Gate*
- *Jack In The Dust*
- *Jack At The Lodge*
- *Jack In The Garden*
- *Jack Fell Down*
- *Jack In Clink*

Other Books

Writing A Crime Novel

Books by Derek Smith

All my books, other than the *Jack of All Trades* series and *Murder at Any Price*, are written under the name Derek Smith.

Fantasy
Hell's Chimney
The Prince's Shadow

Other Books
Strikers of Hanbury Street (short stories)
Catching Up (poetry)

Young Adult Novels
Hard Cash
Half a Bike
Fast Food
Frances Fairweather Demon Striker!

Children's Novels
The Good Wolf
Feather Brains
Baker's Boy

For Younger Children
The Magical World of Lucy-Anne
Lucy-Anne's Changing Ways
Jack's Bus

About the Author

I live in Forest Gate in the East End of London. In my working life, I have been a plastics chemist, a gardener and a stage manager before becoming a professional writer. I began with plays, working with several theatre companies, and had a few plays on radio and TV, as well as on the stage.

In the early 80s I became involved in running a co-operative bookshop and vegetarian café in Stratford, where I learned to cook, and had my first go at writing a novel. The first was a mess, and, after too many rewrites, binned. The transition from drama to novels took me a couple of years to get to grips with.

My first success was a young adult novel, *Hard Cash*, published by Faber. Buoyed up by this, I stuck with children's work, did school visits, and made a hand to mouth living as a full time author, topped up with some evening class work in creative writing at City University and the Mary Ward Centre in Holborn. A few adult fiction titles appeared from time to time, between the children's list, and I have since been working more in that direction with my *Jack of All Trades* series.

DerekSmithWriter.com

The book you've been reading
was designed by Lia
at Free Your Words...

lia@freeyourwords.com